Runaway

Cheryl Zach

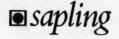

This book is dedicated to one of my most cherished friends,
Marcella Fletcher, who as teacher and then attorney has touched
many lives and helped some of the lost children.

First published in the UK in 1996 by Sapling, an imprint of
Boxtree Limited, Broadwall House, 21 Broadwall, London, SE1 9PL.

Published by arrangement with The Berkley Publishing Group,
a division of The Putnam Berkley Group, Inc., New York.

ISBN: 0 7522 0236 7

Printed and bound in Great Britain by
Cox & Wyman Ltd., Reading, Berkshire.

A catalogue record is available from the British Library.

Chapter 1

Dear Diary,

This is going to be the worst day of my life, but I have to do something. I couldn't sleep at all last night; I lay in bed listening to the spring rain rattle against the windowpanes. I thought about how cold and wet it would be outside, with no home and no bed and no blankets. What will I do if my dad kicks me out?

I'm sure I'm pregnant now. I threw up again this morning, and I haven't had my period for three months. I've got to talk to Seth, but how can I get him a message if my dad won't let me out of the house? I wish we had a telephone like normal people. I wish this family was normal!

How much longer can I keep my dad from noticing? I'm sure my stomach is rounder, already. Should I tell him? I get so scared when I think about that, my stomach goes into knots and my mouth dries up. I almost can't breathe.

Falling in love with Seth was the best thing and the worst thing that's ever happened to me.

I need to talk to Seth!

'Cassie, Mom says come and wash the break-fast dishes, right now,' ten-year-old Mark said from behind her. 'You writing in that dumb diary again? How come you're always writing things down? Let me see.'

Startled, Cassie dropped her pencil. She hadn't heard her brother come into her bed-room. 'Touch my diary and you'll be sorry. Tell Mom I'm coming.'

'Tell her yourself.' Mark stood on his tiptoes and tried to peer over her shoulder.

Cassie shut the cheap notebook quickly. She wished she had a real diary, with a lock on it. She always kept her diary hidden – there were too many younger siblings in their small house and too little privacy. 'Go on, get out of here,' she said. 'I've got to get dressed.'

Not until he stamped out of the room, frown-ing, did Cassie push her diary back under the mattress of her bed and open the closet door, trying to find something to wear that would but-ton at the waist. Her fear returned as she rum-maged through the faded cotton dresses. For once she didn't regret the fact that her dad wouldn't let her wear jeans and T-shirts like the friends she'd once had in school. When would her father notice her rounded stomach, her broadening waist? Her mother should have been the one to pay attention, but her mom lived in her own world, and had done so as long as Cassie could remember.

Sighing, Cassie pulled her long dark hair into a ponytail, and hurried downstairs. Her mother stood at the plain wooden table, kneading bread dough. The breakfast dishes had been stacked sloppily in the sink.

'Don't you want something to eat?' her mom asked in the soft flat tone that was all Cassie had ever heard her mother use. Sometimes Cassie wished that her mother would yell, scream, laugh loudly, anything to show that she was really here, aware of what was happening around her. How did her mom manage to see only what she wanted to see?

Cassie looked at the dried-up egg yolk sticking to the white plates and shuddered, feeling her stomach roll. Swallowing hard, she shook her head. 'I'm not hungry.'

Her mother didn't answer, just continued to knead the dough in rhythmic motions, her pale blue eyes far away. Her graying brown hair, lighter than Cassie's, had been pulled into its usual tight bun, and her dress was loose-fitting and long, cloaking any contour of her body and almost touching the floor. She wore no makeup. Her brown lace-up shoes were similar to the ones Cassie wore; old lady shoes, she thought resentfully.

'Can I walk down to the store after I finish the dishes?' Cassie turned on the hot water and squirted cleanser into the sink. Holding her breath for her mother's answer, she dipped the first plate into the sudsy water.

'What for?'

'I thought you might need something, and I'd like to get some fresh air. The rain's stopped.' Cassie picked up a dishrag and rubbed the dirty plate so hard that it almost slipped out of her hand.

Her mother shook her head without looking up. 'Your father will go on Friday.'

Cassie inhaled sharply, disappointment a heavy weight inside her. 'But I want –'

'Your father said you're to stay in, after lying to him the way you did.' Her mother continued to knead the bread, never varying her steady rhythm.

'Don't I ever get another chance? I haven't been out of this house for two months!'

'Your father said after you were meeting that boy on the sly, he can't trust you.'

'He's not that boy – he's Seth, and he's a good person, if you'd take the trouble to find out. What do *you* think?' Cassie demanded, turning so suddenly that the soapy plate in her hand hit the side of the sink; she heard the crack as it shattered into pieces. Shards of china fell to the floor, but Cassie ignored them.

'Your father says –'

'That's all you ever say! You sound like a tape recording,' Cassie shouted. 'Don't you have any opinions of your own? Wouldn't you like to wear nice clothes and watch a movie or listen to music – just hang out with friends? Wouldn't you like to have friends? I would, Mamma.'

Cassie stared at her mother's face. 'Mamma?' Her mother wouldn't meet her eyes. 'Wives should be subject to their husbands,' her mother said very softly, continuing to knead the whitish dough. She patted the mound tenderly, as if it were a baby. 'Your father just wants what's best.'

'Don't I have anything to say about what's best for me? I want to see people, Mamma. I want to go back to school; I want to go back to church. Why can't we go to church anymore, just because Pa argues with every preacher?' Cassie thought of the last three churches they had been to – she'd liked the one with the youth group; they'd had skating parties and raised money for the homeless shelter. She'd made friends there. Now she couldn't see anyone, even Seth. Especially Seth.

She thought of Seth's arms around her, and felt an almost physical ache for his love, his reassurance. Seth cared; Seth wouldn't abandon her because she was pregnant.

She was sure of it, absolutely sure of it, but

she needed to talk to him, to tell him – he didn't even know that their stolen afternoon was going to change her life. Oh, Lord, Cassie thought. We're always praying to you; my dad talks to you as if he knows everything you want. Can you listen to *me*, to Cassie? What am I going to do?

'I want to know what you think, Mamma. Don't you care what happens to me?'

'Of course I do,' her mother said.

'What if I did something Pa didn't like, what if he were really angry, what would you do?' Cassie held her breath again, willing her mother to look at her, to see her, to see how much she hurt, and how deep was her fear.

But her mother hit the dough with a smack and didn't look up. 'You wouldn't do that; you're a good girl. You've always been a good girl.'

Blindly Cassie bent to pick up the pieces of broken crockery. She couldn't see well; the tears in her eyes made everything blur, and she jerked as the sham fragment sliced her finger. But that was the least of her pain.

Cassie left the sinkful of soapy water and went to the bathroom to find a Band-Aid, dried her hands and shook off the drops of blood. She wrapped the plastic bandage around her throbbing finger, then blew her nose and wiped her eyes. Crying wouldn't move her mother any more than shouting.

Why can't she see what's happening, Cassie thought. Shoulders sagging, Cassie went back to the kitchen and, without speaking to her mother again, finished washing and drying the dishes. Her cut finger smarted when the hot water seeped past the bandage, but she hardly noticed.

By the time Cassie had finished, her mother had the bread dough in a large bowl and had set it on the back of the stove to rise. She wiped the flour off the table and called the three younger children into the kitchen. 'Time for school.'

Ruth and Esther soon bent dutifully over the table, copying Bible verses in their shaky script, while Mark was given a sheet of fractions to add and subtract.

'Show me how to do this one, Cassie,' her brother said, shoving the paper toward her.

Cassie sighed and took the pencil. 'Look, this part is the denominator.

She went through the problem with him, but Mark shook his head. 'This is hard. Do the whole page for me?'

Her mother didn't seem to hear his request. She had picked up her knitting from its basket and sat down in the old rocking chair in the corner of the kitchen.

Cassie shook her head. 'You'll never learn if you don't try it yourself,' she told him.

Mark's eyes narrowed, and his tone was

angry. 'It's too hard. Anyhow, you're just a girl. You're supposed to do what men tell you – that's what Pa says!'

Cassie ignored him; that kind of illogic wasn't his fault, everything came back to their father. She looked down at the worn black Testament her mother had placed ready in front of her.

Instead of opening the Bible, Cassie folded her arms and stared defiantly at her mother. 'I won't.'

'You're still memorizing Leviticus, Cassie,' her mother said as if her daughter hadn't spoken. 'Your father assigned it and he'll be back soon.'

It was an implied threat, but Cassie still refused to open the book. 'Why should I memorize which meats are unclean and how to diagnose leprosy? What's the point?'

'Your father says –'

'This is all so stupid.' Cassie stood up abruptly, pushing the old wooden chair back so suddenly that it tilted, hitting the floor with a bang. The younger children stared at her, the little girls wide-eyed, Mark's expression still resentful, refusing to sympathize.

'I want to go back to school.' Ignoring the fallen chair, Cassie turned and leaned against the cold panes of the window. She stared at the wet bushes, the gray sky past the backyard fence. 'There's a whole world out there, and we're ignoring it. I want an education.'

'The world is an ungodly place, your father says,' her mother murmured, knitting needles clicking industriously.

'I know, I know. The public schools are ungodly, too. But to call this home schooling –' Cassie waved at the bare table. 'Jennifer in my old youth group was doing home schooling, but her family used textbooks and a computer and library and museum visits. This is a joke. I don't want to be some ignorant freak all my life!'

Her mother didn't answer; Cassie didn't really expect it. But from the corner of her eye, she saw the children tense, and turning quickly, she saw her father standing in the doorway, sawdust from the small cabinet shop behind the house dusting his brown coverall.

The room was silent, and Cassie felt her stomach knot. She tried not to tremble.

'I can't believe that a daughter of mine is disdaining the Lord's word.' Her father spoke slowly, in the deep, low voice that had impressed her so when she was younger, when she thought that her father was God, or very close to it. Samuel Sneed stood over six feet, and his hands – the same hands that shaped and smoothed the wood panels that he fashioned into cabinets – were clenched.

Cassie felt light-headed with fear. She'd never before stood up to her father – it was unthinkable. But desperation drove her, and maybe years of frustration. It was her sporadic glimpses of school and church that had showed her families where everyone had opinions, where everyone had value. Not like her family. This time she wouldn't give in.

'Of course not,' she said. 'But I know most of the Bible by heart, already. And there's so much more. You wouldn't let me study *Macbeth* because it has witches in it, you wouldn't let Mark read *Tom Sawyer* because Tom lied to his aunt. I can't read *Cinderella* to the girls because of her fairy godmother.'

'Magic,' her father said, his dark brows knitting, 'is the work of the devil.'

'It's just a fairy tale. You think *Cinderella* is the work of the devil? And so are science books and computers? I don't believe that,' Cassie said. She had to swallow hard at her father's expression.

'You will honor your father and your mother,' her father repeated, his voice even deeper. 'I just want to keep you safe. You don't know the evil that exists in the world. You're not old enough to judge these things.'

Once he had made her feel safe, sheltered against the unknown world outside, protected by his big frame and loud voice and the certainty of his views. But she'd had a few peeks at a bigger world, and it didn't look much like her father had painted it. And she wasn't a little girl anymore.

'I'm sixteen; when do I get old enough to have an opinion? I feel as if you're putting me in a box – why can't I know what other people think? Why are you the only one who knows what God wants?'

Her father took a quick step forward; Cassie flinched, her arms folded protectively over her stomach. But he didn't lift his hand, though his voice was hoarse with anger.

'You will do as I say, Mary Catherine. This is sinful! Think of the example you're setting for your brother and sisters. You should be ashamed. Don't you want to be a godly and proper wife like your mother?'

Cassie bit her lip, throwing a quick glance at her mother, her head still bent low over the flashing hypnotic needles.

No, she thought. I don't want to be like my mother. Aloud, she said, 'I'll never be anyone's wife because you'll never find anyone suitable for me to date.'

'That's what this is about, isn't it?' her father's voice rumbled. 'That boy I've forbidden you to see. He's no good, Mary Catherine. He led you to lie to your father, neglect your work. You'll not keep company with a heathen.'

'You think everyone's a heathen,' Cassie argued, trying to keep her voice from trembling. 'I met him at the church youth group, for crying out loud. Seth's a good person; you'd find out if you gave him a chance. Why won't you agree to meet him? Just because he wore a T-shirt with a rock group logo on the front, and you saw him holding my hand –'

'You will not talk back to me! Go to your room and pray for your sins, and I will pray for the scales to fall from your eyes,' her father shouted.

Ruth made an almost soundless whimper, and Esther ducked her head, eyes wide and frightened. Their mother didn't seem to hear any of it. Only Mark grinned a little, flashing his sister a triumphant glance.

The fierceness of her father's voice made her knees weak. The loudness of it beat against her, almost a blow in itself. Blinking back tears, Cassie moved blindly toward the doorway.

'I want to hear no more from you today,' her father continued. 'Not a word till you can remember your duty to your father.'

'She'll just write it all down in her diary,' Mark muttered beneath his breath.

But the whisper was too loud; her father stopped in the drafty hall instead of turning toward the backyard and the cabinet shop. He stiffened; a wave of crimson rose slowly up from his neck to flush his face, and his dark eyes glittered.

'Keeping secrets? Is Satan working within you?' He headed toward the narrow staircase.

'No!' Cassie ran after him. The fear inside her mushroomed, like the old nightmare where she tried to run and seemed caught in an invisible bog, her feet barely moving. But this was real, and even more horrifying.

She stumbled on the worn treads, almost falling, grabbed the railing beside the stairs, and pulled herself erect. By the time she reached her bedroom doorway, her father was already pulling out drawers from her bureau.

Fear clutched her throat and held back any protests. She watched him dump clean, patched underwear and dull shapeless sweaters onto the floor. When he found nothing there, he turned to the bed. In an instant he had pulled aside the blankets and sheets, lifted the mattress, and found the blue notebook.

He opened the book and began to read.

Chapter 2

Dear Seth:

My father found my diary, and he read it. He knows I'm pregnant; he knows about us, the few times we met secretly. I thought he might kill me; he had an expression on his face I've never seen, and I've seen him angry many times. He burned my diary and made me watch –' Secrets are the devil's work,' he said, and then he locked me in my room.

I think he went out. I can see the backyard from my window and he didn't go to the cabinet shop, but I heard the children later fighting with each other, and no one makes noise when Pa is in the house.

I don't know what he's up to, but I hope he doesn't come after you – I don't know what he would do. He's very strong – be careful. If I can find a way, I'll mail you this letter.

I wish I could talk to you. It's making me crazy, not being able to see you. I wanted to tell you about being pregnant, but not like this. I

don't know what to do, Seth. I love you so much.
  Cassie

Cassie folded the rumpled sheet of paper and put it back into her pocket. She'd reread it and refolded it so many times since she'd written it that the creases in the paper were almost torn. She had no envelope and no stamp, and though she'd written it a week ago, she'd had no chance to try to get the letter into the mailbox. What must Seth think – it had been so long since she'd seen him, talked to him. Would he think she didn't love him anymore? Would he be angry, hurt?

Oh, Seth, she thought, her arms wrapped nervously around her body, hugging herself as she rocked back and forth on the narrow bed. Don't give up on me, Seth. I love you; I need you – you're the only thing I've got. Wait for me, Seth.

She heard the heavy stamp of her father's footsteps on the stairway; she tensed. She heard him stop in front of her door, heard the rattle of the old-fashioned key in the lock, saw the door swing open. She braced herself. If this was to be another session of loud prayer and exhortations to repent, she'd rather he just yelled one more time. But to her bewilderment, her father did neither.

'Come along,' he said. 'We're going out.'

'Out?' Cassie stared in astonishment. 'Out of the house? Where?'

He didn't answer. He pointed, and she walked numbly down the steps and past the kitchen, where the younger children sitting dutifully at the table stared at her. Her mother stirred something on the stove.

'Momma?' Cassie begged.

Her mother didn't look around, didn't seem to hear her plea.

Her father paused long enough to take up a thick brown sweater and thrust it at her. Cassie took it numbly and followed him out the back door – they never used the front, which was double-locked – and past the cabinet shop, which had once been a garage, to the thin gravel patch where the old car sat.

It had been so long since she had been outside that she felt strange walking across the patchy grass and climbing into the old Chevy. Her father shut the door and walked around to the other side of the car. The air was cold; Cassie pulled the sweater on, though she disliked its scratchy roughness and drab color.

'Where are we going?' she demanded. She felt numb and afraid; her father wouldn't really abandon her somewhere on the streets, would he? Her hands trembled at the thought. 'If your eye offends thee, pluck it out,' the echoes in her mind repeated. It was her father's deep voice that resonated in her memory.

Her father turned the key in the ignition, and the motor sputtered, then the car moved jerkily out into the street. Still, he didn't answer.

Cassie clutched her cold hands together in her lap to stop their shaking. This didn't seem real. She watched the streets slide by and felt as if she peered into another world. She saw small houses, a trailer park, a discount store with big windows, and people in brightly colored clothes walking and talking and laughing. She saw two girls her own age getting on a school bus, wearing jeans and red and green jackets, their hair stylish, earrings dangling.

Cassie felt a wave of loneliness – where was Seth? Already at school, walking along the halls beside girls like that, pretty girls who could call him up, go out with him anytime he asked? How long would he wait for her, with no word?

The old car rattled on; they passed the grocery store, the hardware store, drove on downtown, and her father parked in front of the courthouse.

'What are we doing?' Cassie demanded.

But her father wouldn't answer; he opened the car door instead and motioned her out. Gripping her arm just above the elbow, he pulled her along, and she almost ran to keep up with his long strides. The ugly sweater swung open, and she felt the chilly breeze cut through her thin cotton dress. Then they were inside a hallway, through to an anteroom, being directed into an inner office.

A short, stout woman sat behind a desk. Her auburn hair was cut short and her suit jacket unbuttoned, showing a white blouse underneath. Her eyes were intelligent behind narrow-rimmed glasses, and the desk in front of her was piled with books and papers.

'This is Mary Catherine Sneed? Won't you sit down, dear. You can wait outside in the outer office, Mr. Sneed. This won't take long.'

Cassie blinked to hear anyone tell her father what to do.

Her father frowned, but to her surprise, he walked back out the doorway, leaving the door open. She saw him sit down on a chair in the hallway, as if standing guard, while his eyes watched her.

The woman in the green suit got up and walked around her desk, shutting the door firmly.

Cassie looked at her.

'I'm Ann Wade, your juvenile officer. Do they call you Mary Catherine?'

That at least she could answer. Cassie said hoarsely, 'Only my father calls me Mary Catherine. My mother – doesn't call me anything, much. My friends, when I had any, called me Cassie.'

'Cassie, then,' the juvenile officer said. 'Do you understand why you're here?'

Cassie shook her head slowly.

'Your father has filed a petition with the juvenile court, asserting that you are unruly and out of control.'

'Out of control?' When she couldn't even leave her house? The craziness of it made Cassie want to giggle, but the woman's expression was too serious.

'He says you've lied to him, that you've been dating a boy he doesn't want you to see. He says you're pregnant; are you pregnant, Cassie?'

Her tone was matter-of-fact, but Cassie flushed and stared at the worn beige floor beneath her feet.

'Cassie?'

'Yes,' she muttered.

'I see.' The juvenile officer sighed and opened the file in front of her, the pen in her hand moving across the page.

'Will they put me in jail?' Cassie whispered, the old nightmare returning in a new form.

Ann Wade looked up quickly. 'Oh, no, Cassie. If you're sent away, it would probably be more like a school, a boarding school – it's not a jail.'

But Cassie couldn't seem to concentrate. The woman's words floated away in a noisy buzz, and Cassie's ears roared with her own fear. She gripped the arms of her chair tightly; the juvenile officer was saying something about a hearing, about her rights – she couldn't make sense of it, the buzzing in her ears was too loud.

'Do you have any questions, dear?'

Cassie shook her head again; asking a question would mean making her brain work, and her tongue, and both seemed frozen.

'We'll see you tomorrow then; try not to worry.'

But Ann Wade was opening the door, and her father waited outside. Cassie felt swept along like a piece of trash in a rain-filled gutter, pushed by the current toward the dark sewer ahead, riding helplessly toward the blackness.

The rest of the day was a blur. Her father took her home, put her back in her room – she even had her meals there, now – maybe he thought she'd infect the rest of the family, Cassie thought bitterly. Pregnancy wasn't contagious; after so many children, didn't he know?

She didn't sleep that night. The next day, to her bemusement, the whole family crowded into the old car and drove back to the courthouse. This time she sat in the center of the backseat. Her brother, in his coat and white shirt, wearing a tie like their father, sat stiffly on one side; the little girls were crammed into the other corner. Cassie felt trapped, suffocated.

When her father parked the car, she thought once about running – she didn't know where exactly, running to find Seth, to beg him for help – but her father gripped her arm again, as if she were too feeble to walk unassisted, and she was swept along through the wide doors.

This time they didn't go to an office but on to the second floor to a courtroom.

A young man in a suit waited outside the double doors, his arms full of files and papers. 'Are you Mary Catherine Sneed?'

Cassie's father made to brush past him, but the young man stood his ground.

'Excuse me, Mr. Sneed, but I'm the public defender assigned to Mary's case; I need to speak with her privately before we go into the courtroom. You folks can go ahead and take a seat inside.'

Cassie's father looked ready to argue, but the solemnity of the courthouse seemed to have impressed even him. Reluctantly he let go of Cassie's elbow, and the rest of the family filed into the courtroom.

Cassie looked at the young man. He seemed hardly older than her high school classmates; his suit jacket was set awkwardly on his narrow shoulders, and his necktie was crooked.

'You're a real lawyer?' she asked doubtfully.

'Passed the bar three months ago,' he said proudly. 'Arthur Booker, at your service. You can call me Art. What should I call you – Mary, Kathy?'

'Cassie,' she told him. 'What's going to happen to me?'

'That depends on the judge's ruling. I would have liked to have seen you sooner, but I've got such a backlog of cases . . . But you have to tell me, Cassie, how do you plead?'

'Plead?'

'Guilty or not guilty to the unruly charge. Have you refused to obey your parents?'

'My father says I have,' she mumbled. 'But it wasn't fair. All I did was try to see Seth; my dad wouldn't let me out of the house.'

'And you're pregnant?'

She nodded, flushing.

'So you did see him, I take it?' His tone wasn't unkind, but Cassie bit her lip.

'Only once or twice.'

'Once is all it takes.' He shifted the load of paper in his arms and pulled the door open. 'They're calling our case. We've got to go in.'

Cassie wanted to run the other way, not walk through the wide doorway. But the young attorney waited, holding the door, and she walked slowly into the big room.

Cassie felt numb with fear. She looked at the flags draped on the wall, and the tall, wide desk that loomed up in front of her. The judge wore a black robe; she thought wildly that he looked even more godlike than her father.

Ann Wade was there again, this time in a

beige suit, sitting at one of the front tables. She nodded to Cassie. Another older man stood in front of the big desk, talking to the judge.

The public defender took a seat at one of the tables and motioned to Cassie to sit down. Cassie felt very cold. She sat on the hard wooden chair and tried not to shiver.

The other man walked back to his table and picked up some papers. His voice was crisp and full of authority. 'Your Honor, we're here to present a petition filed against this young lady, Mary Catherine Sneed. Samuel Sneed states that his daughter, Mary Catherine Sneed, sixteen, is unruly and beyond parental control. She has lied to her parents and refuses to submit to their authority. She has met and cohabited with a young man whom her father feels is a bad influence, and as a result she is now pregnant.'

Everyone was looking at her, the judge from his seat, the man with the forceful voice, the juvenile officer, another woman at the front of the court, her family. Cassie shut her eyes. She wished she could disappear, wish this all away, make it all a bad dream. Everything – everything except Seth. She wouldn't give up Seth.

They called her father to the stand, and he said all the things he had said to Cassie, except he didn't shout this time, and his face didn't turn red, and when he said, 'I only want to protect my daughter,' it almost sounded true.

Then they called her mother to the stand. Cassie tensed; it was somehow harder hearing her mother's listless voice repeat the list of accusations than it had been with her father.

'And did she shout at you, Mrs. Sneed, and refuse to do her schoolwork?'

'Yes,' her mom said without looking at Cassie.

You should have been on my side, Cassie thought with a flicker of anger beneath her despair. You know what Pa's like; you know.

Then it was her turn.

Feeling somehow detached from her body, Cassie was surprised that she could even walk to the witness stand. It felt like a hundred miles. She was so scared that she could hardly see the people seated in front of her. She was nervously aware of the judge to her right, as if he were a dog about to bite.

'Do you promise to tell the truth, the whole truth . . .

'Yes.' Her voice sounded strange, wispy as a bit of morning fog.

The public defender spoke first. 'Do you feel that your parents are overly restrictive?'

'What?' Her mind wouldn't work; how could she explain with all these strangers watching her? They had already made up their minds, she knew it. She stumbled through her story, but when the young lawyer sat down, and the other man stood up again, Cassie trembled. His gaze was stern, like her father's.

'Your father says that you have yelled at your mother, you've frightened the younger children, you've neglected your studies and refused to cooperate in your home schooling.'

It wasn't fair, Cassie thought. Her father had twisted everything around. But she thought of the time she had shouted at her mother, and under the man's stern gaze, she couldn't argue.

She looked across the aisle toward her mother, sitting motionless in the second row, her hands folded meekly in her lap. The little girls sat beside her, dressed in white-collared print dresses carefully sewn by their mother, and their faces were white and frightened. Even Mark, who had marched into the courtroom standing rigid and straight like a younger version of their father – Mark the favored child, the boy – now looked uncertain.

'Mary Catherine, are these statements true?'

'Not exactly,' she whispered.

'Speak up, please, so we can hear you. Did you yell at your mother?'

'Only once,' Cassie said.

'And refuse to do your assigned schoolwork?'

'But it was stupid –'

He didn't seem to hear. 'And you did, in fact, meet with a boy whom your parents asked you not to see, and you had sex with him, and you are now pregnant.'

She stared at the floor.

'Is this correct, Mary Catherine?'

'Yes,' she muttered.

'Just one more question. Have you ever thought about running away from home?'

Startled, her daydream of running to find Seth flashed through her mind. How did this stranger know her thoughts? Cassie felt blood rush to her face. Blushing hotly, she couldn't answer.

'Remember that you're under oath, Mary Catherine,' the judge spoke suddenly. She glanced at him. His eyes were the color of steel, gray tinged with blue. He was portly and balding, but the black robe made him look like one of the avenging angels that her father was always preaching about. 'Please answer the district attorney's question.'

'Sometimes.'

'That's all. You can step down.'

Somehow, she got back to her chair and sat down in a fog of confusion. The lawyers talked some more, then for a few seconds the room was silent. The judge rubbed his balding head, then spoke.

She had missed something. Cassie pulled her gaze and her attention back to the judge. 'Sadly, I find it necessary to sustain the petition . . . Because of the flight risk . . . for your own good,

I think it best to remove you from your home. McNaughten Home for Girls is in East Tennessee, near Knoxville, but I think it's the best facility

It was really happening; this wasn't just a bad dream. Cassie wanted to scream. She looked back at her family – they seemed already very far away. Cassie willed her mother to speak up, to protest, to stand up for her oldest child. But her mother stared down at the hands clasped tightly together in her lap and said nothing.

Her father sat with his arms folded, his expression complacent. He didn't even look at Cassie; he was watching the other children instead. They looked scared and bewildered. It was because of them, she thought suddenly, not just her, that her father had done this. Her brother and sisters would never forget what could happen if they crossed their father. They would be punished, like their big sister, sent away into the outer darkness, with wailing and gnashing of teeth .

And Seth didn't even know. She heard scraps of the judge's voice, but couldn't concentrate. She heard him say something about her education, about proper medical care, and instinctively she touched her swollen abdomen. But nothing mattered now. She was being sent away, and she hadn't even seen Seth to say good-bye.

'Sorry, Cassie,' Art told her. 'It may work out, you know.' He tried to arrange his pile of papers; one drifted to the floor and he bent to find it, then stood up with his arms full.

The juvenile officer touched her shoulder gently. 'Cassie, do you want to say good-bye to your family?'

'What for?' Cassie muttered.

The hearing seemed to be over; she heard a door close somewhere. The district attorney stood and chatted with the public defender. Just another day's work, she thought numbly. The judge had left his high seat, and her family waited in the aisle. She didn't want to look at her mother, or her father's satisfied smile. Her sisters were crying, and her brother's face was white.

'Cassie, I'm sorry,' Mark called to her.

She reached to hug him quickly, put her arms around the little girls, then stepped back. Ann Wade guided her toward a far door, not the one they'd come in, and Cassie felt her whole life slipping away. She was walking into the unknown, and she'd never been so afraid.

She almost couldn't see, but she followed the juvenile officer blindly and presently found herself in another office. While the adults around her conferred quietly, Cassie sat at a small table. It was scattered with paper, and she suddenly focused on a blank envelope.

She reached out and touched it gingerly, then looked around, but no one seemed to notice. Cassie fingered the envelope, then felt for the folded, wrinkled sheet of paper that she still carried in her pocket.

She saw a pencil on top of another file. She picked it up, wrote Seth's address on the front of the envelope, scribbled a few lines at the top of her letter, then thrust it inside. When the juvenile officer came back to her, holding a small bag that Cassie recognized as her mother's old suitcase, the woman smiled.

'The van's ready to leave, Cassie. I don't want you to worry; you're going to like it at McNaughten, honestly. You'll be able to finish high school, and you'll get prenatal care. This is for the best, I think.'

Cassie swallowed hard; she hardly recognized her own voice, it sounded so hoarse. 'Would you do something for me, please? Would you mail this for me? I didn't have time to say good-bye. I don't have a stamp, but –'

The juvenile officer's brown eyes were kind. 'Of course. Have a good trip, Cassie.'

And they took her away.

Chapter 3

Dear Cassie,

I miss you so much. I wish I could see you. Why won't your dad listen to me? Did he tell you I came to your house last Tuesday and tried to talk to him? It was my second try; the first time he wouldn't even open the door.

I stood outside on the step and tried to tell him that I'm not a bad guy, that I'm not out to hurt you, that I love you more than life — but he shut the door in my face, yelled at me never to come back. He looks a little crazy sometimes, Cassie, when he yells like that.

I don't know what to do. It's driving me nuts, not being able to talk to you, make sure you're okay. I went to the community center and the library every night last week, and to the grocery store every afternoon, hoping you might be there, but no luck. Won't he even let you out of the house?

Things aren't so good here, either. I think my mom is really serious about this Dan guy, and

*he's a creep. I don't know how I'll stand it if I
have to live with him all the time.*

*I wish I could see you. I'm going to mail this
letter and hope you can get to the mail before
your dad – if he finds it first, he'll probably burn
it, or something. I love you, Cassie, don't forget
that.*

Seth

Someone opened the door behind him. Seth
hastily folded the paper and shoved it into an
envelope. He put the envelope into his jeans
pocket until he could find a stamp and turned to
see his mother standing in the doorway. She
frowned and took a quick puff on her cigarette.

Seth tried not to cough; he'd struggled with
asthma all his life.

'This place looks like a pigpen; didn't I tell
you to clean it up?'

'It's my room,' Seth said, glancing over the
unmade bed piled with dirty jeans and T-shirts.
He saw a few tapes on the floor, school papers
lost in a pile of *Sports Illustrated,* and a damp
towel or two. 'It looks lived in. Maybe I like it
like this.'

'Yeah, and it's my apartment, Mr. Smart
Mouth, and you can get this stuff cleaned up,
now.'

'The living room doesn't look any better.'

'So you can't pick up the living room, too?

Think you're too good to help out, now that you are seventeen? Don't get too big for your britches, mister. I'm the one who fed you and bought you clothes and dragged you to the doctor every other week – remember that before you talk back to your mother.' She took another quick, nervous puff.

'The doctor said I wouldn't be there so often if I didn't live with a smoker,' Seth said, but he lowered his voice. His mom looked ready to start yelling, and he didn't enjoy the kind of scene that would follow.

She either didn't hear or ignored his comment, pushing her tinted, reddish hair back from her face and looking at her watch.

'Get your tail in gear. Dan'll be here soon; I don't want him to think we live like pigs.'

'Why not? He'd fit right in.'

This time she did hear, and her face flushed. 'And what's that supposed to mean? Don't be so stubborn. Can't you give him a chance?'

'He's a jerk,' Seth said, refusing to meet her eyes. He bent over and picked up his tapes, stacking them neatly on the crowded bureau.

'You don't like anyone I like,' his mother complained. 'You never do.'

'Mom, listen to me.' Seth tried to meet her eyes, but she looked away, taking another nervous puff from her cigarette. 'I'm afraid he won't treat you right. This guy's mean, I can see it in his eyes. What if he knocks you around, like that salesman you dated last year? You deserve better than that.'

'Dan's different. He's a fun guy. Stanley was a loser, I should have seen that coming.' His mother seemed to remember that she shouldn't be smoking in his room; she waved uselessly at the blue cloud that hung over her cigarette. 'Anyhow, that's ancient history, now.'

Seth thought that his mom had too many men in his history, then felt disloyal for the thought. But she glanced at him again and seemed to read something in his expression.

'Don't be such a little prude.' Her voice rose. 'Don't you think I have a right to a life? Just because your dad took off when you were a baby, you think I should sit home alone till I die? I'm not an old lady yet, and I'm not sitting on a couch knitting just because you don't approve of my boyfriend.'

Seth winced; the frantic note of self-pity, almost panic, that crept into his mother's voice was worse than the anger. She had too much makeup on again, and her skirt was too tight. She was pretty without all that stuff, with her red hair and full lips, but she didn't seem to believe it.

'Forget it. I'll clean the place up,' he said. 'Don't stress, okay?'

She stamped out of the bedroom. In a

moment he heard the clink of bottles in the tiny kitchen past the living room; the apartment was so small that every sound carried. How would Seth be able to tolerate living with Dan, who seemed to dominate the whole place when he was here? What if his mom's boyfriend moved in full-time?

Seth felt his shoulders tense just at the thought. He walked into the living room, picked up the empty glasses and the newspaper scattered over the floor, plus some torn panty hose his mom had abandoned on the couch. The place did look bad, and Seth didn't mind helping out. His mom worked nights at a local restaurant and she was always tired and grumpy from lack of sleep, but he hated cleaning up for Dan. He hated Dan, period.

As if on cue, he heard someone bang on the front door of the apartment. The doorbell was broken, and the landlord wouldn't get around to fixing it.

Seth wished he could ignore it, but his mom had already heard. She hurried past her son and pulled open the door. 'Hi, honey!'

Seth refused to look around, but he heard the sound of a noisy kiss, laughter, murmuring. When he finally looked up, his arms full, he saw the big man staring down at him with an expression of disdain.

'Hi, kid. Glad to see that you're doing something to earn your keep.' Dan was a big man, his neck wide, his face round. Seth's mom thought he was good-looking. Seth thought Dan's grin never seemed to reach his eyes.

'Yeah,' Seth said now and headed for the kitchen to dump the glasses in the sink and the rest of the stuff in the garbage can. He heard Dan say from the other room, 'Too bad he's such a wimp, Maria. Now if I had a kid, he'd be like his old man – a football player, popular at school, a fun kid, you know?'

'Seth tried out for football when he was a freshman,' he heard his mom answer, almost apologetically. 'But he was sort of thin, and his asthma, you know

Seth grimaced. It made him feel bad enough to watch his mother acting like a teenager on her first date. Now she was making excuses for him. And the football – he loved sports, he'd always wanted to play on a team. But he was allergic to several pollens, and they didn't have enough money for the weekly allergy shots. He'd thought he was doing pretty good in the tryouts until the first time he'd tripped and fallen running down the football field, then the wheezing had begun The coach had been nice about it, but it was no deal.

He'd thought about trying out for the team again; his asthma wasn't as bad as he grew older, Seth told himself, but it still caused occasional attacks. And he didn't want another pat on the head, another 'Nice try but no cigar.' So Dan thought he was a wimp, just because he didn't make the football team? How was he going to live with this guy? Would his mom marry him?

Seth lingered in the kitchen, absentmindedly restacking the dirty dishes in the sink. He was in no hurry to go back into the living room, where Dan had taken over the couch, his mother snuggled close beside him.

Maybe Seth had been a sickly little kid, with eyes too big and a wheezy voice – not exactly a prize. His dad must have thought so, too. He'd left home when Seth was five and hadn't been heard from since. No child support, as his mom always reminded Seth, no indication of any concern for his son. Maybe by this time his dad had another family somewhere, with sons who were big and strong and played football, who didn't have to carry an inhaler around in their shirt pocket, just in case.

When Seth was little, and the other kids had made fun of him for not being able to run as fast or as far, he'd longed for his dad to come home. Sometimes there were men around he liked – one boyfriend of his mom's had seemed to like him, even playing catch with Seth a few times, but he hadn't stayed around long, either. There'd been a third-grade teacher he admired, and then the O'Halleys, a neighbor and his wife who had fed him milk and cookies after school, listened to his stories when his mom was still at work or too tired afterward, even came to his school and admired his posters and his science projects. Maybe Seth wasn't a football star or a basketball whiz, but he could do some things well, if anyone cared to notice.

He'd made good grades once in a while, too, but missing so much school had put him behind.

He missed the O'Halleys. They were the ones who'd taken him to church, where he'd met the kids in the youth group he still attended occasionally. But Seth's mom couldn't keep up the rent on the house, and he and his mom had moved to a smaller place, then moved several more times, and though he tried at first to visit the old couple, they'd retired across state to be closer to their married daughter. He got postcards from them sometimes, but it wasn't the same.

Since the O'Halleys had left, no one had made Seth feel special, made him feel loved and appreciated, not until he'd met Cassie. Cassie was a gift, unexpected, like the golden egg you find in the Easter egg hunt just when you've about given up, and all the other kids have run ahead, laughing because you're left with an empty basket.

Cassie was a treasure.

Seth thought for the thousandth time about how soft her brown hair was, and how lovely her hazel eyes. Her voice was soothing, like a love song, and she had a way of looking right into his eyes that made him think she could see into his soul.

The first time he met her at the church hall, he'd been entranced. The more he saw her, the more Seth knew he loved her as he'd never loved anyone before and might never love again. Cassie made everything else bearable; he could think about her at school and at home and while he worked at the restaurant after school stacking dirty dishes and busing tables.

They'd talked for hours at the back of the church hall, about their secret dreams, about studying and traveling and seeing new sights together. With Cassie holding his hand, Seth could almost believe in all of that, could almost believe that someday they would visit New York and London and Paris, like Cassie dreamed of. How her eyes shone when she spun those dreams. And most of all, to have a future together, a home, a marriage, children – those thoughts made his heart swell with new hope and pride.

When her dad wouldn't let her attend the youth group anymore, they'd been desperate. Not being able to see Cassie – it made Seth's fists clench, just thinking of the loneliness of it.

After she'd been forbidden to go out to the church, he'd met her at the community center in the afternoons or walked her home from the grocery store. Then one afternoon he'd had a bad spell with his asthma, and she'd come up to his apartment, worried about him.

And what had happened then, they hadn't planned, hadn't been prepared for. Not that he could be sorry – remembering the feel of Cassie lying in his arms, becoming one with him – it was a little bit of heaven, Seth thought now, tingling with the memories. But they'd had no protection to use; he'd never bought a condom and they hadn't expected to make love, had never talked about sex, and now he was worried about Cassie. He hadn't seen her in two months – her dad apparently wouldn't let her out to go anywhere – and Cassie hadn't been to school for over a year. Seth couldn't talk to her, couldn't even look at her from across the room. Missing Cassie was like an ache inside him.

The giggling had stopped in the living room; maybe it was safe to go back in. Seth looked at the rooster clock on the wall; it was almost time for his shift at the restaurant.

He walked back through the living room, glancing swiftly at the two on the couch. His mom had lit another cigarette, and Dan had perched his on the side of the overflowing ashtray. Smoke hung over the couch like a malevolent gray cloud; Seth felt the warning tightness in his chest; he had to get out of here. He picked up his jacket from the chair.

'Got to go,' he told his mom. 'I'm on at four-thirty.'

She nodded. 'Darn right. Tom said you'll get fired if you are late again; you punched in late twice last week.'

He'd gotten behind because he'd been hanging out in front of Cassie's house, hoping to see her, but he couldn't tell his mom that.

'Got to be dependable, kid,' Dan told him. 'Me, I'm always on time at the plant – they set their watches by me.'

'Good for you.' Seth turned toward the door. 'Not interested in your mail, Smartass?' Dan called after him. 'I picked it up on my way in, I'm such a nice guy.'

Seth turned so quickly that he almost tripped. 'Mail? For me? From who?'

'Probably got his mind on some girl,' Dan told his mom. 'No wonder he's been slacking off at work. Needs a lesson, your kid does.'

Seth stared at the small envelope in Dan's big grip. 'Give it to me. It's mine. Mom!'

His mother looked uneasy. Dan patted her shoulder. 'Go on and put your earrings on, Dumpling, touch up your lipstick. I'll talk to the kid. We need to get to know each other better, right?'

Seth watched uneasily as his mother stood up and headed for her bedroom, her high heels clicking on the scarred parquet floor. She pulled the door shut behind her.

Seth lifted his chin, watched Dan watching him. 'Give me the letter,' he said, reaching.

Dan's arm was longer, and his grip too hard; he pushed Seth back easily. 'Think you're so smart, don't you, kid? I got news for you. When I move in, no question who the boss around here will be. You got that?'

Seth frowned. Then his stomach tightened as Dan pulled a lighter from his jeans pocket, flicked it, moved the dancing flame beneath the letter in his other hand. Seth held his breath.

'No, don't!'

'You understand me, kid?'

'Yeah, yeah, you're the boss. I get it. Just give me my letter. Please.'

Dan grinned. He waited one more agonizing second; the envelope was turning brown. Then he flipped the lid shut on the lighter and dropped the smoldering envelope.

Seth grabbed it, beat out the flame, and hurried out the door. He turned the corner and plummeted down the staircase. Not until he was two flights down, his chest hurting from his rapid flight, did he dare to stop and pull out the damaged letter.

It was from Cassie, as he'd thought. He read it slowly.

'*Dear Seth,*' it said. '*They're sending me away . . .*'

Chapter 4

Dear Cassie,

I read your letter three times. I couldn't believe it. How can they take you away like this? You're the only thing in my life that's good, that makes me want to get up in the morning. I can't live without you, Cassie.

It makes me crazy to think of you unhappy and so far away. Your letter sounded so hopeless. And a baby – our baby. I won't let you down, Cassie. I won't let them do this to you. I don't know how, but I'm going to find you, get you out of that place.

I love you, Cassie. Wait for me. I'm coming for you.

Seth

He folded the letter carefully, wishing he could put it into Cassie's hand himself, put his arm around her, wipe the tears off her cheek. Thinking of Cassie alone and afraid, far away from home, made something inside him swell with anger and fear until Seth thought he might explode.

And he was going to be a father. Seth tried to picture himself holding an infant, remembered the squalling babies he'd seen at the mall, or in the restaurant where he worked after school. He thought of parents trying to quiet fussy toddlers and wailing, well-wrapped bundles. It didn't seem real.

He shook his head. The baby wasn't here yet. Cassie was the one who needed him now. He had to find her. She'd put the name of the girls' home in the letter, near Knoxville she'd said, but he didn't know the address. How could he find out?

He grabbed his jacket and headed for the stairs. He dug into his jeans pocket; he found only three crumpled dollar bills and a handful of coins. He'd given his last paycheck from the restaurant to his mom; she'd said she was short for the rent money. He'd have to borrow some from her to buy a bus ticket to Knoxville.

He thought about taking the bus down to the courthouse, but it was only a couple of miles, and he might need the money, later. So Seth walked, instead. The sky was clouding up, and the wind cut through his jeans. It blew crumpled sheets of newspaper along the sidewalk; he pushed one away, kicking a stray soda can that rolled into his path.

Seth shivered and pulled his jacket collar up, pushing his hands into his pocket. He thought about Cassie; where was she right now? Already in Knoxville? On the road somewhere, lonely and frightened?

The thought of her alone and afraid caused a physical pain, an honest-to-goodness pain in his chest, it hurt so much. Hang on, Cassie, he thought, I'm coming.

The courthouse parking lot was almost deserted; Seth hurried through the old-fashioned double doors and scanned the list of offices posted on the wall. He didn't want to register a car or pay property taxes. He wasn't buying a marriage license, either, though for a moment he had a wild fantasy, seeing Cassie standing by his side, smiling, as they signed their names on a piece of paper, ready to marry, to tell everyone else to leave them alone and let them be together. Oh, Cassie, he thought again.

He saw JUVENILE JUSTICE on the signboard and forgot the daydream. Third floor. He ran for the elevator, found two men in dark suits waiting before the closed doors, and an elderly lady on crutches. Too impatient to wait, Seth ran for the stairs.

He was panting by the time he reached the top, and he felt the usual tightness in his chest. The sign above the door said JUVENILE JUSTICE; the door was of frosted glass.

The door was shut, and a woman was turning a key. Horrified, Seth called, 'Wait, wait, I need to ask a question.'

She opened the door for a moment and stared at him through the crack. 'It's five o'clock; we're closed.'

'But you can't be! I need someone to tell me where McNaughten Home for Girls is. I need to know the address.'

She gave him a long look. 'And why do you need the address, young man?'

'I . . . I have a friend there, I want to write.'

'You can talk to the juvenile officer tomorrow; I can't give out any information.' She shut the door while Seth tried to protest.

'But –' The key clicked in the lock.

Head down, he leaned against the door. The glass felt cold against his forehead. If he put his fist through the glass, would anyone listen? No, that was a stupid idea.

Seth swallowed hard, but the lump in his throat wouldn't budge. He couldn't wait until tomorrow. Who else would know the address? Her family, of course, but Cassie's dad would never speak to him. Seth had tried that already. Could he catch her mom alone at home?

He had to try. Seth clattered back down the steps and set out again. The streetlights were on now, and most of the offices and small shops downtown were closing. A few people hurried along the sidewalk, heads bowed against the frosty wind. Cars filled the streets, full of people going home from work, home to their families.

Seth didn't have a family, not really. All he had was Cassie, and they'd taken her away.

It took him almost an hour to get to Cassie's street, with its row of little houses, some neatly painted, some run down. He stood outside and looked for signs of life – the house could have been empty, almost. A light shone in one back window, but he heard no hum of a television, no music playing. Weird people, Cassie's family, he thought.

He walked up and down in front of the scraggly yard, deciding what to do. The front of the house was so blank, maybe he should try the back. But how could he escape the attention of her father?

Seth walked around the corner of the house, saw the small building to the rear that Cassie had told him was now her father's cabinet shop. He could hear sounds of banging from inside the workshop.

Great, maybe he could find her mother at home and talk to her privately. Seth ran toward the back door and knocked gently.

For a moment he thought no one had heard. Looking uneasily over his shoulder toward the workshop, Seth knocked again, then waited impatiently until the door opened.

A faded-looking woman in a sagging gray sweater and cotton dress stood in the doorway; she looked at him in surprise.

'We don't want any,' she said and moved to shut the door.

'I'm not selling anything,' he said quickly. 'Please, I'm a friend of Cassie's; can you tell me where she is?'

Her mouth twisted. Seth saw that her eyes were red-rimmed and swollen. 'You're that boy, the one who got her into trouble, aren't you? You should be ashamed!'

'I love her, honest,' Seth said, the words rushing out, all jumbled together. 'We didn't mean – I never thought – I need to find her, tell her –'

'You stay away from Cassie,' her mother said. 'You've caused enough trouble!'

She slammed the door, and Seth took a step backward. He felt a drop of rain, then another. But he ignored the drops hitting his face, running down his cheeks like tears. No one would tell him how to find Cassie; what was he going to do?

A small sound warned him. Seth looked over his shoulder and saw the big man who had yelled at him the last time he came here, a stick of wood uplifted, ready to swing.

Seth ducked, his heart racing with fear, and jumped aside.

The man swung again. 'You're a demon in disguise,' Samuel Sneed shouted. 'Misleading my poor little girl!'

Seth ran, almost slipping on the wet grass, heard footsteps behind him, and rounded the corner of the house.

He was younger and faster, even with his asthma, and Cassie's father couldn't keep up the pace. Seth stopped at the end of the block and looked over his shoulder, gulping for air as he waited for the tightness in his chest to ease. The older man had turned back, disappearing behind the house. Seth was still in one piece, but he hadn't learned the address of the girls' home.

He'd go anyway; someone in Knoxville must have heard of it. Maybe it was on a city map; did they put places like that on a map, like hospitals and schools?

He couldn't wait for tomorrow to try the juvenile office again; they might not tell him, anyhow. It was as if the whole world was against them, determined to separate them. But Cassie needed him, he knew she did.

Seth wouldn't give up. He trudged home in the rain, his sneakers sodden by the time he climbed the stairs slowly to his apartment.

He opened the door with his key and headed for his bedroom, pulling off his dripping clothes, wiping the water off his face, and rubbing his hair dry with a towel. He pulled on a dry T-shirt and jeans, found a sweatshirt to put under his damp jacket.

To his surprise, he heard the front door open. He went to look. 'Mom?' What was she doing home at this hour?

She had on her waitress outfit, and her expression was stormy.

'Where the blue blazes have you been? You just got yourself fired, you know that? Not turning up for work, not even calling. How could you do that?'

Seth groaned and leaned against the door frame. 'I'm sorry, Mom. I forgot.'

'You forgot. I thought maybe you'd been run over by a car. And you forgot. We needed that money, mister. Where's your head, Seth Allen? It's sure not on your shoulders.'

Her mascara had run, leaving dark circles under her eyes, and she had a smudge of lipstick on her upper teeth. Seth couldn't help thinking of Cassie, and how fresh and pretty she looked with no makeup at all.

'Mom, I'm really sorry. I'll look for another job, okay. But I'm in a jam. Can you lend me some money? I gave you my last check for the rent, remember? I don't have any dough.'

'You should have thought about that before you flushed a good job down the toilet. I don't ᵥave money to throw away. You're not buying ᵣre you?'

'I'm not stupid.' Seth frowned at her. 'Not that stupid, anyhow. But I need –'

'You need, you need, what about what I need? What about helping me by keeping your job. You're going to be just like your father.' She pulled a tissue out of her apron pocket and blew her nose loudly.

'No, I'm not!' Seth shouted back. 'I'm not.' He couldn't face the fury on her face, the disappointment. And he had to get to Cassie. He turned and started toward the front door.

'You get yourself down to the restaurant,' his mother yelled after him. 'Tell 'em you're sorry, you were sick, anything. Try to get your job back. Do it, you hear me!'

Seth slammed the door behind him, but outside he paused to lean against the wall. His stomach churned, and he couldn't seem to think. Somehow, some way, he had to get to Knoxville.

His mother caught up with him outside the apartment, her jacket and purse hanging haphazardly over her arm. 'Come on,' she said, taking his acquiescence for granted. 'You can ride with me; I gave up my break to come check on you. Now I won't have time to eat all night; as if I didn't have enough to worry about.'

He followed her down the stairs, guilt now layered on top of his anxiety and anger and frustration. Again, Seth felt the seething inside him, like a volcano with pressure building. He held on to his temper with great effort.

'Listen, Mom, I'm sorry about the job. I'll find another one somewhere as soon as I can.' He thought she looked a little calmer. 'But about that money –'

They had reached the parking lot, and Seth climbed into the passenger side of the old Buick. It started with a shudder and a groan, and his mom pulled the car into the road.

'Not that many jobs in a town this small,' she was complaining again. 'And it's not like you're an A student, is it?'

'Nope,' Seth agreed morosely. 'Just your average moron, that's me.'

'You be real nice to Tom at the restaurant, and maybe he'll give you another chance. You got to work on your smart mouth, Seth. Learn to get along with people. Like Dan. Whether you like him or not, I do.' She glanced nervously at him, then back to the road. 'He's moving in with us next week. I need help with the rent now, even if I didn't have other reasons, which I do. So you just keep your mouth shut and don't give him a hard time, you hear?'

Seth folded his arms, staring hard at the dashboard. His nightmare was coming true. Living every day with that jerk – just great.

'He doesn't like me,' Seth muttered.

'He'll like you fine if you act nice,' his mother

told him. When she pulled the car in behind the small restaurant, she turned off the engine, twisted the rearview mirror, and fussed with straying wisps of her hair, then opened the door. 'It'll work out, you'll see.'

His whole world was falling apart, Seth thought. The wet parking lot glistened with reflections of the restaurant's lights, but his own personal darkness seemed almost overwhelming. He had to force himself to walk into the back door. His mom hurried on through the kitchen and into the dining room.

Another busboy stood loading plates into the big dishwasher. He threw Seth a sympathetic glance and nodded toward the supply room. Seth found the manager checking a list against a shelf of boxes and cans.

'You finally decided to show your face, huh? You know what time it is, Allen? If you've got some dumb excuse, you can forget it. I got no jobs for kids who can't show up on time, can't be depended on.'

'But I can,' Seth argued, knowing this was a wasted effort. 'I had an emergency, that's all.'

'Sure. Get out of here, kid. We got work to do.'

So much for apologies. It didn't matter. He'd find another job later; right now, he had to think about Cassie.

How was he going to get to Knoxville if his

mom wouldn't lend him enough money for a bus ticket? He thought briefly of their old Buick, but the car was barely running; it might not make it that far. Besides, he couldn't steal his own mother's car.

He walked back toward the parking lot, his hands in his jacket pockets, his shoulders drooping. Time was passing, and every second, every minute, took Cassie farther away from him.

He wasn't undependable; he would not be like his dad; he wouldn't. He would take care of Cassie; he would get her out of this place she'd been forced into. He had to do something quickly.

He heard the rumble of a large engine and looked up to see a big rig parked at the side of the lot. The driver was just turning on his lights.

Suddenly inspired, Seth ran across the blacktop and waved his arms at the driver.

'Hey! Which way you going?'

The driver lowered his window halfway and looked cautiously down at Seth. 'East.'

'Can you give me a ride to Knoxville? I need to get there in a hurry.'

The man shook his head. 'Sorry, kid. I'd get fired. Insurance won't let us pick up hitchers, too many hijackings, you know?'

'But –' Seth watched in frustration as the man rolled his window up and pulled the big eighteen-wheeler out of the lot.

Then he heard footsteps behind him. 'Where you trying to go, sonny?'

Seth turned. The man had a wrinkled, suntanned face, denim overalls, a faded baseball cap on his head. 'Knoxville. You going to Knoxville?'

'No, but I could take you partway. What's the rush?'

'Uh, someone sick, my grandmother. I don't have the money for a bus ticket.'

'What about your folks?' the old man said, his eyes shrewd despite the wrinkles that fanned out from their corners.

'I don't have any family.' Seth almost believed it. His mom had a new boyfriend; nobody would miss him if he was gone. The only person who needed him was Cassie, and he had to find her, help her.

'I got some stops to make, but I can take you as far as Cookeville, if you want.'

'Th-thanks, thanks a lot,' Seth stuttered, his relief almost overwhelming.

'Hop in, then.' The old man walked across and opened the door to a battered gray pickup truck almost as ancient as its driver. The truck bed held several bales of hay, a sack of animal feed, and a German shepherd mix that looked at Seth suspiciously as he approached the truck. The dog growled, and Seth felt his whole body go tense.

'Easy, Bobo,' the man said. To Seth, he added, 'My burglar alarm, in a manner of speaking.'

To Seth's dismay, the dog jumped out of the back of the truck and leapt ahead of the old man into the center of the seat. The man climbed in behind the steering wheel, and nodded to Seth to go round the other side.

Seth frowned, but he opened the other door and, under the dog's disapproving gaze, slid cautiously onto the edge of the seat. The animal showed its teeth silently, but didn't reach for him, though Seth braced himself. He'd been bitten by a dog once, when he was seven. But he'd ride with a cage full of tigers to get to Cassie.

'Let's go,' Seth said.

Chapter 5

Dear Diary,

They gave me a stack of notebooks for my classes, and I kept one to use as a diary. I still miss the old diary that my father burned; without somewhere to write down what I'm thinking, I might go nuts. I've never felt so alone, and I don't know who to talk to.

The drive up seemed to last a lifetime, yet it ended too soon. When we drove through the gate and I saw the black iron fence, I thought sure this would be a jail, no matter what they had told me. The house is brick, nicer than my house, at least what used to be my house. I don't feel I have a home anymore; I feel lost, like an abandoned puppy.

I miss Seth. I hope he got my letter.

Cassie heard footsteps in the hall and closed her notebook quickly. Was this her roommate? Cassie had arrived at McNaughten with a sore throat and slight fever, and had been sent straight to the nurse where she had to endure a complete physical. Finally, the middle-aged woman had read the thermometer, swabbed Cassie's throat, peered into her ears, and patted her on the shoulder.

'Had a stressful few days, have you? No surprise you should catch a bug.'

So Cassie spent the first night alone in the infirmary, with a button to call the nurse, then the next morning was pronounced well enough to be assigned a room. Now she sat curled up on one of the two beds that occupied each end of the dormitory-style bedroom.

The girl who walked into the room had a pretty face, smooth skin the color of coffee with cream, and dark hair in neat corn-row braids. Her lips were tinted, and dangling earrings hung at each ear. She looked at Cassie with hard eyes, and she didn't smile.

'You the new girl, huh? What's your name?'

'Cassie.' Cassie clutched her notebook, bracing her shoulders against the other girl's unfriendly stare. 'Are you staying here, too?'

'Darned straight. That's my bed over there.' She pointed to the bed with the bright red spread. 'And my bureau, and my stuff in the closet. And you don't touch nothing of mine, girl, or you be sorry.'

Cassie blinked, watched the other girl throw her shoulders back, put her hand into one jeans pocket, wiggle her fingers beneath the denim.

'I got a knife, see. I'm tough. You don't mess with me, girl.'

Did she really have a knife, or was she bluffing? Cassie had no desire to find out; she swallowed hard, wishing she were anywhere but here.

To Cassie's relief, a knock at the door made them both pause. A woman in her midthirties came in. Her dark-skinned face wore a friendly smile, and her dark hair was cut short. She smiled at them both.

'Hello, Angela. I see you've met Cassie; I'm sure you're going to help her feel at home.'

Angela pulled her hand out of her pocket quickly, pulling her purple sweatshirt down low. She didn't meet the woman's eyes, studying her purple nail polish instead. 'Yeah,' she murmured.

'Cassie, I'm Mary Sue Porter, one of the counselors here. Would you like to come to my office so we can have a chat?'

'Okay,' Cassie said, glad for any excuse to get away from the belligerent Angela.

She followed the counselor into the hall, down a wide set of stairs to a small office on the ground floor. Cassie looked around. On the bookcase sat a framed photograph of Mrs. Porter, a dark-skinned man in a suit and tie, and two small kids, everyone grinning. A framed college diploma hung on the wall, next to a poster of a rainbow.

The counselor waved her to a chair at the corner of the desk and sat down herself, looking at a folder that lay open on the desktop.

'Mrs. Porter, do I have to stay here?' Cassie blurted. 'Am I in jail?'

'It's not a jail, Cassie,' the counselor said patiently. 'The court feels that a controlled situation is in your best interests. It won't be so bad here.'

Sure, she thought Angela was a friendly roommate, too, Cassie thought glumly. But the counselor was still speaking.

'I've requested your files from your last school, Cassie. You've been home-schooled for the last year, is that correct? Could you tell me what you've been studying?'

'Just Bible readings, which I already knew,' Cassie said. 'Nothing about schoolwork.'

The counselor looked thoughtful. 'That's a shame. I understand from the court report that your father's been summoned to Family Services to discuss his lack of proper procedure about the schooling. But you're here now, and we can get you back on track.'

Cassie brightened. 'Is there a library here? Do you have books to read?'

'Of course, we have a small library in the building, and you'll have access to the school

and public libraries, too. Lots of books, Cassie.'
Mrs. Porter smiled at the change in Cassie's
expression. 'Do you like to read?'

'Oh, yes. I love it, but my dad – he wouldn't
let me read books anymore, or go to the library.
And I like school, too. I was pretty good in my
classes. I'd like to go back to school.' Cassie felt
some of her depression lift; the weight on her
shoulders seemed not quite as heavy.

Mrs. Porter chuckled. 'That's a wonderful
attitude, Cassie. I think you're going to do just
fine. Now, I'll tell you a little about our
schedule. We have a group counseling session
once a week that I'd like you to participate in.
I'm also available if you need to talk privately.
We'll plan your class schedule in just a minute,
and I'm going to see about getting you some
clothes; we have some maternity clothes in our
communal clothes closet. They've been used
before, but they're still in good condition. But
first, we have some serious questions to think
about. What do you plan to do after the baby is
born?'

Cassie blinked. She looked away from the
counselor, stared down at the floor. 'I don't
know. We didn't mean to do it, any of it, and I
never thought about a baby.'

'But it's a fact, now,' the counselor said
gently. 'The physical confirmed that you are
pregnant, almost sixteen weeks. You have some

serious decisions to make. Will you give the baby up for adoption, to a stable, loving couple ready to take care of a child? Or do you plan to keep the baby?'

'They would let me do that, keep it, I mean?' It hadn't occurred to Cassie that she could decide. All her life her father had told her what to do and she had obeyed, at least until recently, and look what had happened, then. She was afraid to make another decision. And a baby – this was a big choice to make, one that would last forever.

'No one will tell you what to do, but I want you to think seriously about what is best for you, and what would be best for the baby. Have you discussed the options with the baby's father? What does he think? Legally, he'll also have to sign to allow the baby to be adopted. And if you keep the baby, how are you going to take care of it? Would you go back to your parents' house?'

Cassie knew her eyes had widened. She shook her head, hard. 'Oh, no, never; My dad would never let me bring a baby home, with me not married. He thinks I've sinned enough already.'

Mrs. Porter nodded. 'I see. You could qualify for welfare after you leave here, Cassie, but it's not a large amount, and you'd be on your own – that won't be easy, for you or for the baby.'

Cassie didn't answer. There was Seth, she

thought with a glimmer of hope. Seth would want the baby, too, wouldn't he? She should have had the chance to talk to Seth. If she could just see Seth, ask him what they should do . . .

The counselor closed the folder. 'Give it some thought, Cassie. I know it's a big decision. We'll discuss this again later, okay? Let's go down and pick out some clothes for you.'

The trip to the clothes room was fun. Even though the maternity clothes weren't new, they looked good to Cassie, who had spent too much time in the drab dresses her father thought suitable. She found two pairs of loose-fitting maternity jeans, with elastic panels for her expanding stomach, and some cute, brightly colored T-shirts, cut wide and loose, and several sweaters. Mrs. Porter wrote down a list of her sizes and said, after a glance at Cassie's worn, hand-me-down shoes, that she would see about getting Cassie a new pair.

Her arms full of clothes, Cassie headed back to her bedroom. Not until she reached the door did she remember Angela. She'd meant to ask the counselor what would happen if the two couldn't get along. Would the juvenile home throw Cassie out, too, like her father had? The thought brought back the butterflies in her stomach.

She opened the door and went in, ready for anything. But Angela was sprawled across her own bed, flipping the pages of a magazine. She looked much less intimidating, and she barely glanced up as Cassie came into the room.

Cassie went to her own bed, moved her notebooks aside, and looked through her newly acquired clothes one more time. She touched the smooth cotton knit of a T-shirt, examined a soft blue and white sweater. She'd so rarely had anything pretty to wear, and never anything remotely like the clothes the other high school kids wore. It hadn't bothered her too much when she was little, but as she got older, she could feel the other kids staring at her in her drab shapeless dresses, the brown sparrow in the midst of fashionably bright songbirds.

Angela pushed herself up. 'Got you some clothes from the clothes room, huh? You pregnant?'

Cassie bit her lip, but Angela would have found out soon enough, anyhow. 'Yes,' she said shortly.

'Who's Seth? He the papa?' Angela swung her legs around to sit on the edge of the bed.

Cassie jerked her head up. She felt as if she'd been violated. 'You read my diary!'

It was too much. First her father, now this girl she didn't even know. Before she knew what she was doing, Cassie took three long steps across the room and grabbed the other girl by the shoulders. 'You don't touch my diary, you hear me!'

Angela looked startled. Her mouth flew open, and she tried to push Cassie away. 'Don't mess with me, girl. I told you —'

But Cassie was too angry to listen. She shook her roommate once, hard, then released her abruptly and stepped back, still breathing quickly. 'I don't care what you told me. I won't bother your stuff, but you stay out of mine. And never touch my diary, again, I mean it!'

Angela raised dark brows. 'Okay, okay, you don't have to get all bent out of shape.' Her tone was unexpectedly mild.

Cassie turned on her heel and went back to her bed. The sudden outburst had surprised her as much as it had Angela. The old Cassie would never have stood up to a stranger. Sitting down amid the piles of clothes and notebooks, she felt tears suddenly come. She wiped her eyes angrily.

What next?

Chapter 6

Dear Cassie,

I'm on my way, but it's taking longer than I thought. I didn't have enough money for a bus ticket, so I had to get a ride with a farmer. He got sleepy last night, but he wouldn't let me drive, just because I don't have a license. So we slept in the truck at a rest stop and started again this morning. His truck is slow, and he's slower. But I'm trying.

Cassie, hang on. I hope you're okay. I think about you every minute. I wish we'd been more careful; I'm so sorry you got into this mess. It's my fault, too. I should have thought about what could happen, how it might affect you.

But I'm coming to get you, Cassie. I won't let you down.

I love you.
Seth

Seth scribbled the brief note on the back of a yellow sheet of notebook paper he'd found behind his head, in a jumble of trash and old papers behind the truck seat. He put the note into his pocket until he had the chance to mail it. Not that he had the address of the girls' home, yet, anyhow, and he hoped to see Cassie within a few hours. But it made him feel better to write to Cassie, even if he couldn't mail it right away.

Now he waited impatiently for the farmer, whose name was Ollie Rockford, to come back to the truck. Ollie seemed to have a stop every thirty minutes, to pick up supplies, to fill up the old truck or check the tires, to walk the dog, to visit a rest room. 'Kidneys not what they used to be,' he explained solemnly to Seth as he climbed awkwardly back into the truck. 'Body gets old a'fore you know it.'

Seth nodded, trying to be polite, trying not to yell at the old guy for taking so long. With a fast car and money for gas, he could have been in Knoxville already. As it was, they'd just rounded Nashville. Seth had stared at the tall buildings, watched the bustle of traffic on the interstate, and bit his tongue to keep from yelling at Ollie, whose response to the more congested roads was to slow down even more. Cars whipped around them, and Seth wished for any other vehicle but this beat-up turtle.

Finally, they left the state capital behind and headed east on Interstate 40. Seth looked for a road sign, finally found one. KNOXVILLE: 160 MILES.

The rolling hills around Nashville changed as they drove farther into the plateau. The highway sloped upward more now, and the old truck chugged along, slowed by the long, rising grades.

The old man was a talker. 'When my wife died, I decided it was time to slow down,' he told Seth. 'But I couldn't give up the farm; it was Grandpap's first, you see, and he bought it from a cousin. Been Rockford land for a long time. But I only had girls, three of 'em, fine girls, all married now. And nobody wanted to farm. Hard work, farming. You ever worked on a farm, sonny?'

Seth shook his head.

'If I'd had a son, now. But Ben, my oldest grandson, he might want the place someday. So I hold on to it, and keep a few cows, some hens, you know . . .'

Seth nodded while the old man rambled on, hearing all about the three daughters, the grandchildren, all talented and smart and fine-looking, all scattered around the state.

'That there's a picture of Millie's youngest.' The old man pulled out a leather wallet molded to the shape of his back pocket and thumbed through the plastic photo holder. 'He won the school spelling bee last fall, smart one, he is.'

Seth looked at the grinning, snaggle-toothed boy in the snapshot, so plain he was almost ugly. But Seth felt a pang of envy for this unknown kid who had a grandfather who bragged about him, who probably had parents who were proud of him, too, and a father who hadn't left home, a mom who didn't yell, didn't search frantically for another man to bring into her life.

It was the old loneliness, Seth thought. The emptiness inside because no one was there to hold you in the dark when the monsters came. He used to have nightmares and wake screaming, but his mom worked nights and didn't have enough money for a baby-sitter. So he'd been left to sleep alone, restless and afraid, knowing that dark shapes would materialize in his bedroom as soon as his mother walked out the front door.

He wouldn't walk out on Cassie, not like his dad had done. He'd be there for her, hold her hand when she had the baby. They did that now, Seth thought vaguely. He'd seen it on some TV show. They let the fathers watch and help and wear green robes, and Cassie would know that he cared, that he was responsible – no matter what his mom said – that he'd be there when she needed him.

How many miles, now?

Ollie launched on about another grandchild, this one a girl who had fearsome talents with the computer. 'You got a map?' Seth interrupted.

The farmer nodded, put his wallet back into his pocket, and leaned across the dog to open the glove box. It was as jumbled with paper and old gloves and rusty flashlights as the back of the seat, but he found a folded map and tossed it to Seth before slamming the door shut.

The map was frayed at the edges and looked ready to fall apart. Seth unfolded it gingerly and tried to determine their location. There was Knoxville, at the eastern end of the state, and it still seemed a long way for them to go.

He glanced outside at the thickly wooded countryside, the almost empty highway stretching up toward the mountains that lay ahead. Heavily budded trees showed touches of green against their bark, and dogwood were just opening their first brave white blossoms. A mockingbird fluttered along the side of the road, a flash of white showing against dark wings, and once Seth saw a deer hesitate at the edge of the highway.

Seth sighed, feeling the tension in his muscles. Every time the truck chugged and coughed and slowed even more, his shoulders jerked; he wanted to push the old vehicle along, make it go faster, stop the black smoke that belched from the tailpipe as the incline became steeper.

Then the engine faltered; Seth heard the ominous whine with a sinking heart.

'Don't sound good,' Ollie pointed out, unnecessarily. 'Better stop and have a look; hope it's not the water pump again.'

They sputtered along until the next exit, then pulled off the interstate and drove at a snail's pace to the intersection. One small gas station sat on the other side of the connecting road; besides that, Seth could see only trees stretching along the ridgeline. He made out no sign of homes or other businesses, no town within easy reach.

What would he do if the old man couldn't go any farther? Ollie was in no hurry, but Seth definitely was.

They pulled into the gas station, and Ollie got out and opened the hood. While he bent to peer beneath it at the engine, Seth sat inside the truck, tense with impatience, wondering what he could do next.

He folded the map and reached for the glove compartment. The lid fell open, and half the junk inside slid forward. Seth pushed it back. As he did, he touched something with the hard feel of metal. Curious, he lifted a paper, looking for the solid shape he had accidentally encountered. It was a small gun.

Seth looked at it in surprise, touched the end of it.

The dog growled.

Seth shut the lid hastily and stuffed the map in his pocket. 'Hey, relax, I didn't take anything,' he said, trying to make his tone soothing.

The dog still had its bristles raised, yellowed teeth slightly bared.

Seth sat very still. He'd never lost the uneasiness that dogs gave him, though he had only a small scar on his leg to remind him of the childhood assault.

Ollie reappeared around the hood. 'Have to let it cool off,' he said. 'Then I'll see what I can do. Come on, Bobo, you need a walk anyhow.'

The dog didn't move; its black eyes stared at Seth as if it longed for the power of speech, for a way to expose Seth's secret thoughts.

But when Ollie snapped his fingers and pulled open the driver's side door, the big dog jumped down and followed the old man toward the grass and trees at the side of the station.

Seth watched them go. When Ollie had turned away, Seth opened the lid on the glove compartment again and reached deep into the jumbled papers to find the gun. He pulled the revolver out, surprised at its unexpected weight. It was small, but lethal and forbidding. Seth stared at the empty cylinders; where were the bullets? He reached inside the glove compartment again, found a rusty flashlight, a package of crackers, then a box, small and heavy.

Seth hesitated. Looking up, he saw that Ollie had turned and was bringing the dog back to the truck. Quickly Seth slammed the lid shut and shoved the gun out of sight into his jacket pocket. It felt reassuringly hard and heavy in his hand. He squeezed the stock, then pulled out his empty hand and tried to look innocent.

Ollie pulled open the door and the dog jumped inside, staring at Seth with its small dark eyes. The dog knew, Seth thought, feeling guilt written all over his face. If the dog could talk – But Ollie was thinking only of his truck. He slammed the door and went back to stare under the raised hood.

Seth slid out of the truck, shutting the dog inside with relief. He walked around to the front.

'Can I help?'

The old man shook his head. 'Still too hot to touch.'

Seth looked around; he saw a pay phone in its shell-like enclosure at the side of the pavement. Maybe he could call Cassie.

He headed for the small station. A plump woman with frizzled brown hair leaned against the counter. Seth pulled out the crumpled dollar bills from his jeans pocket. 'Can I have change for the phone, please?'

'Sure.' She opened the cash register door, counted out quarters for him, smoothed the creased bills, and put them into the cash drawer.

Seth took the handful of quarters and walked to the phone. The phone book that should have hung on the chain beneath the phone was missing. Sighing, he put in one coin and dialed information.

'What city?'

'Knoxville; I want a McNaughten School, or something like that,' Seth told the operator.

Silence, then the tinny voice returned. 'McNaughten Home for Girls?'

'Yes,' he said quickly. 'That's it.'

She read the listing. Seth found a grubby pencil stub in his pocket and wrote the numbers on a gum wrapper. Then he dialed.

'Deposit three dollars seventy-five, please, for the first three minutes.'

Jeeze, that would take every nickel he had. Seth shook his head and counted out his change carefully. Please, please, let Cassie be there. He felt weak inside, thinking of hearing her voice. The distant ringing inside the phone began; he held his breath.

'McNaughten Home for Girls,' the distant voice said. 'May I help you?'

'I want to speak to Cassie Sneed, please,' he said, trying to sound polite, businesslike, as if the blood didn't drum inside his head till he almost couldn't hear her answer.

'And who is calling?'

'Umm . . .' Seth thought quickly. They might not let her take a phone call from him; he should have thought of that before. 'It's her brother, Mark.'

'Just a moment.'

At least she hadn't hung up on him. But the silence stretched on, and he only had three minutes. Seth held his breath, wanting to shout hurry, hurry.

At last he heard quick footsteps, then Cassie's hesitant voice. 'Mark? Is that you? Did Pa let you call?'

'Cassie, don't say my name. It's Seth. I had to speak to you, Cassie. Are you okay?'

'Oh, oh.' He heard her confusion, then her voice changed, and the sweetness of her tone made him weak inside with longing, with love. 'It's – it's so good to talk to you. It's not too bad here, but I miss you so much.'

'Oh, Cassie, I know. I hate what they did to you. I'm on the way, Cassie, I'm coming to Knoxville, but the truck broke down outside of Cookeville. But I'll get there somehow. I'll get you out; I swear.'

Silence, then she said carefully, 'You don't understand. I have to stay here; they won't let me leave. But there's something else – you know about the baby; they asked me what I'm going to do. I'm thinking about adoption, Se –

Mark. It might be the best thing for the baby, you know?'

Seth felt as if he'd been hit. Take away his baby? Just as it was beginning to feel real, the idea that he would be a father, that Cassie would have his child. 'No, don't do it, Cassie,' he said quickly. 'That's our baby, yours and mine. I won't give it up, Cassie. I want the baby, and I want you.'

'But, how –'

'Deposit two dollars and fifty cents, please,' a mechanical voice interrupted.

Seth gripped the phone so hard his fingers whitened. 'Cassie, I don't have any more money for the phone. But wait for me, I'm coming. I love you, Cassie!' He shouted the last words, and he didn't know if she heard, because the line went dead.

Frustrated, he banged the phone into its receiver so hard that it bounced off again, and he left it swinging on its chain.

How could he rescue Cassie, when he didn't even have enough money for a phone call? No wonder Cassie didn't seem to believe him. Some help he was. Disgusted with himself, with the whole world, Seth wandered back to the truck, where Ollie was peering at the dirty engine, poking at it with a grimy cloth protecting his hand.

'Looks like the water pump is shot; engine's

overheated again. Have to see if they have any auto parts here.'

It was a tiny station; Seth followed Ollie into the store, listened with rising frustration to the conversation that followed. No, they didn't have any parts for the old truck; maybe the woman's cousin could bring a new pump from the auto parts store in Lebanon, but it would likely be tomorrow.

Ollie didn't seem too upset. 'Maybe have to sleep in the truck tonight,' he said, his tone resigned. 'Sorry, kid. Didn't get you very far, did I?'

Seth shrugged. The disappointment was too harsh. 'Not your fault,' he muttered. 'Thanks for the ride this far, anyhow.'

He turned aside and looked at the snack cakes, the chips, the peanuts in the stands beside the counter. His stomach rumbled, it was so empty that it hurt, and he thought about how long it had been since he'd eaten. But he'd used all his money for the phone call, brief as it had been.

He pushed his hands into his jacket pocket and felt the hard shape of the gun. He jumped; he'd forgotten it was there. It was empty; there were no bullets. Ollie would know that, but the old man had wandered back outside and was bending over his truck again.

The woman behind the counter wouldn't

know; there was the cash register, stuffed with bills. Might be a hundred dollars, more. Enough money to buy a bus ticket, Seth thought. He could be in Knoxville tonight, figure a way to get Cassie out of the school, get away together so they could talk about what to do. They could find a way to keep the baby, get married, and make a life together.

Dreams. He was still stuck here in the middle of nowhere, with a truck that didn't run, and no money. And he was keenly aware of the money in the cash register, so close, yet so far.

He fingered the gun inside his pocket, stepped closer to the counter.

The woman looked up. She was short and dumpy, but her faded blue eyes were kind, and she had smile lines around her mouth. 'Want something, hon?'

She was probably someone's mother. He couldn't do it, couldn't hurt her, didn't want the smiling blue eyes to widen in alarm. And what good would it do? She'd just tell the police who had robbed her, and he'd never make it to Knoxville, to Cassie.

'No,' Seth murmured. 'Nothing.'

He walked back outside, sat down on the shaky wooden bench in front of the station, and put his head in his hands. Cassie might as well be a million miles away.

And she was thinking about giving away the baby, his baby.

He had to get to Knoxville.

Chapter 7

Dear Diary,

I'm excited and scared at the same time. I've wanted to go back to high school for months, but now I wonder if the other students will accept me.

Will everyone know that I don't have a real home, that I've been sent away to this place? I feel like a freak. And it's such a large school, nothing like the old high school in my hometown. When Mrs. Porter drove me down yesterday to take placement tests, get my schedule and textbooks, I couldn't believe how big the building was.

I'm so nervous!

Cassie put her diary notebook back under her pillow and stood up to peer into the mirror. Her face looked pale. She pulled a comb through her hair, still damp from the shower, and wished for makeup, though she wouldn't know how to use it. And her dad would say – she pushed that thought away.

At least in her stretch jeans and cotton top, she looked like the other kids, for once in her life. Cassie looked down at her new running shoes and pulled on the denim jacket the counselor had given her. She picked up the stack of books and notebooks and headed for the hallway. She'd been told to meet the other high school students downstairs at the front door of the school.

Angela was there, and half a dozen other girls. Cassie looked around nervously.

'Are you waiting for the high school bus?'

'No,' Angela answered, her tone sardonic. 'I'm on my way to Hollywood to get rich and famous. What'd you think?'

A couple of girls giggled, and Cassie bit her lip.

'I thought there would be more, that's all.'

Angela raised her dark brows. 'Some of the girls are on home-bound, and the junior high kids go in half an hour. What's the matter – don't you like my company?'

'Sure,' Cassie murmured. The truth was, she would have liked more people between them. The two girls had shared a tense peace since Cassie's explosion yesterday – an outburst she remembered with surprise. She'd buried her anger and resentment for so long that to see those emotions emerge still made her feel as if she were watching another person.

The yellow school bus rolled into the driveway. One of the home's counselors watched as the assembled students filed out the door and down the walk; the woman waved cheerfully as they climbed the steps to the bus.

Cassie felt strange as she followed the rest of the girls into the vehicle. She'd never ridden a school bus before. When her dad had allowed them to attend the local public schools for varying periods before he'd pulled them out again, he'd always taken them to school himself. With her father looming over her as they walked into the building, she'd never had a chance to stop and talk, or laugh with the other groups of kids. Making friends had been hard, when she had looked so different from everyone else and had switched schools so often. And she could never invite anyone home or visit another girl's house. She'd only been allowed to go to church, and that had soon been forbidden, too.

Now she hardly knew how to behave. She walked down the aisle, too nervous to meet the eyes of any of the students already seated on the bus. Finding a seat empty halfway back, she slipped in and sat down. The vinyl seat felt cold through her jeans; she clutched her pile of books very tightly.

The bus pulled out of the drive and back into the street; the kids on the bus resumed their chatter. Did everyone know where she and the others lived, and why? Cassie stared at her lap, not sure how she would ever fit into the crowd who laughed and joked around her.

When she finally lifted her eyes, she saw Angela two seats away, staring out the window, her expression wistful. In front of Cassie, a short, stocky boy had turned to give her an appraising glance.

'We got a new one, Ed. Stacked, too.'

His eyes lingered on the T-shirt visible beneath her half-open jacket, and Cassie fought the urge to fold her arms protectively across her chest. Her breasts, swollen by the effects of her pregnancy, suddenly felt too big. She felt her cheeks burn.

'Looking for some fun, babe? You're one of the bad girls, right? Let me tell you, you get bored in that place, I'm the guy to see.'

The boy sitting beside him snickered, and the laughter spread as kids in the nearest seats joined in.

Cassie stiffened. She felt as if the name of the girls' home was branded across her forehead. She didn't know what to say. Still blushing hotly, she shook her head and looked away from his knowing eyes. She wished desperately for Seth, Seth who was gentle and kind and never embarrassed her. Why couldn't it be Seth she was riding to school with, instead of this jerk?

She kept her eyes fastened on the view past

the dusty window. Shops and apartment buildings flashed by, and cars and trucks crowded the lanes. Even on the outskirts of Knoxville, the streets were much busier than she was accustomed to; the small town that she'd left didn't compare to this.

The bus jerked to a stop in front of an apartment complex, and a plump girl with braces sat down beside her. Cassie thought about trying to speak to her and went so far as to smile shyly.

But her seatmate had already turned to continue a conversation with a girl on the other side of the aisle and didn't seem to notice.

More stops soon filled the bus to capacity. Sighing, Cassie rode the rest of the way in silence, feeling very much alone. When the bus pulled up in front of the school, she was glad to be released from the crowded, alien atmosphere. Would school be this unfriendly, too? Cassie gathered up her books. As soon as the girl beside her stood up and moved away, Cassie hurried up the narrow aisle toward the door.

But she took only a step before stumbling over an unseen obstacle. Losing her grip on her books and notebooks, Cassie dropped the whole load and fell forward on top of her new textbooks.

She felt the impact on her elbows and knees, and heard a shout of laughter nearby. Flushed, she pushed her long hair back and looked up to see the stocky boy still chuckling.

'Too bad,' he said. 'Guess you didn't see my foot in the way, huh?'

'Should be a law against feet as big as yours, Mally,' someone else said, and this time it was the boy who reddened as laughter rang out again.

To Cassie's surprise, it was Angela who held out a hand to pull her up, Angela who bent to help her gather up the books and notebooks that lay scattered on the floor of the bus. And under cover of the laughter around them, it was Angela who muttered to the boy in the next seat, 'Do that again and I'll break your jaw, Smart Boy.'

He stopped laughing.

Cassie bit back a grin and followed Angela out of the bus. As they walked across the black-top toward the school building, she rubbed her sore elbows where the fall had scraped them. 'Thanks for the help. Why'd you do it?'

Angela shrugged. 'You're such a baby, somebody has to look out for you. Besides, I don't want him pushing you around – might hurt the kid.'

Cassie stared at the dark-skinned girl, surprised. 'You'd care?'

'You think I'm some kind of monster? I've got a baby, too, you know.'

Shocked, Cassie stopped. Angela kept walking and, after a long moment, Cassie hurried after her.

Angela's glance was quizzical as Cassie caught up. 'Shut your mouth, girl, a truck might drive through it. You know where to go?' They had walked through the double doors of the twostory building.

'I'm not sure,' Cassie admitted. 'Are we in any of the same classes?' She realized that she sounded hopeful. Amid the noisy crowded halls, where the unaccustomed clatter of conversation, playful shouts, and banging of locker doors made her tremble, where all the faces were strange, Angela suddenly seemed an old friend.

The other girl glanced at the textbooks Cassie held. 'English, chemistry, world history, algebra – I don't think so. What's your first class?'

Cassie dug the sheet of paper out of her jeans pocket and read the room number aloud.

'You're on the second floor; I'll show you,' Angela said. 'What's your locker number?'

'Twenty-one twenty-five.' Cassie clutched the schedule tightly, as if it were a good-luck charm.

'That's down the hall from your first class,' Angela explained.

Cassie followed her up the wide staircase, brushing past students and an occasional teacher, almost dropping her armload of books when someone pushed too closely past her. How would she ever keep up with these students who'd been to a real school all their lives? She'd look like a fool. Cassie almost wished herself back in her parents' kitchen, sitting at the bare wooden table where no one would call her stupid, think her out-of-date and ignorant.

But they had reached the classroom; Angela pointed. 'In there. I got to go.'

'See you at lunch?' Cassie asked.

'Don't push your luck,' Angela said. 'I got my own friends, white girl.'

Cassie felt her smile wobble.

'Hey, I'll see you on the bus this afternoon,' Angela said, her tone less belligerent. 'You be cool, hear?'

'Sure,' Cassie agreed, trying to control the knots in her stomach. She took a deep breath and entered the classroom.

Where was she supposed to sit? Cassie looked around the half-filled room; the other students were talking and flipping through notebooks. Cassie saw a girl applying lipstick, another checking her hair in a small handheld mirror.

Vanity, her dad would say. The devil's work. Cassie thought the girls looked pretty. Did wearing lipstick really mean you would go to hell? Her dad seemed far away right now, but she still heard echoes of his voice in her head.

Defiantly she took a seat behind the girl with the lipstick and put her books down on the desktop. Cassie stared at the posters on the wall; she saw European cathedrals and mountain ranges topped with snow. Was that the Alps? A model of a castle sat in the back of the room, with several globes, and a long bookcase over-flowed with books. Cassie felt her fingertips tingle – she wanted to spin the big globe with the multicolored countries, touch the books lovingly. She sensed a whole world opening up to her, and for an instant forgot her fears and savored the richness of it, the sheer luxury of knowledge.

Maybe the other kids, the teacher, might think she was stupid. But here she had a chance to read and to learn, to prove herself. Her dad had thrown her out; the judge had ordered her away. But for the first time, Cassie felt a rush of excitement. The dark box that had imprisoned her had opened, and she was seeing daylight for the first time in a long while. She felt like a plant slowly lifting its head to a long absent sun.

'You finished that report, yet?' the girl in front of her said to a classmate across the aisle.

Cassie's nervousness returned, and her excitement faltered. She'd be behind the class, coming in the middle of the school year. How would she ever catch up with them? But she took a deep breath, refusing to admit defeat before she'd begun.

Even if the kids here didn't like her, even if they treated her like the boy on the bus – she hoped fervently he wasn't in any of her classes – she still had the chance to read, to learn, to step into a bigger world, the real world.

The teacher came into the room; he was a big man, and for a moment, Cassie trembled. He looked like her father. She had to swallow hard, blink back the panic. But when her vision cleared, she saw that he had a narrow face and longish blond hair, with mild blue eyes that gazed at her now in inquiry. He looked nothing like her father, after all.

'Hello there. Do you have an admissions card for me?'

She remembered the pink card in her textbook that she'd been instructed to hand over to the teacher. Cassie pulled the card out. Despite the weakness in her knees, she walked to the front of the room and handed the card over silently.

He scanned the information. 'Mary Catherine Sneed.' To her relief, he didn't say the address aloud, though he must know the girls' home, know what it signified about her. 'What do you like to be called – Mary?'

'Cassie,' she said quickly, finding her voice. 'I'm Cassie.' She liked him already.

The rest of the day passed in a glorious blur. Cassie forgot to worry about the other students. She had books, books that her father had denied her for months, a wealth of books.

Even at lunch, when she had to face the large cafeteria with its deafening clamor of clinking utensils and too-loud voices, she had a book under her arm when she went through the line, took the plastic tray with its pizza and salad and fruit, handed the white-garbed lady at the end her lunch card. Then she could find an empty seat at the end of a long table and nibble at her food while she finished a chapter. She had a lot to catch up on – it felt like her whole life almost – though she'd been out of school only a year this last time.

After lunch she went to English and was alarmed to find that the students were writing an in-class essay. The teacher, a tiny, birdlike woman, seemed to sense her panic.

'Just give it a stab,' she said quietly, pushing back a strand of gray hair. 'I don't expect you to be perfect the first day, you know. I'll give you a week, at least.'

Cassie almost gasped until she saw the humorous glint in the teacher's eyes. Then she grinned in response and sat down at an empty desk. The topic written on the blackboard was 'The Value of Friendship.'

Cassie didn't have any friends. No, there was

Seth; he was her friend, and so much more. She remembered the afternoons when he would rush from the high school to the community center, and how she would time her visits to coincide with his. Walking into the big common room, he would be waiting for her, and the whole room seemed to sparkle. She never felt nervous with Seth; he would listen so patiently to her when she talked. He never laughed, never said 'impossible' when she confessed her deepest dreams. And he told her she was pretty, even in her oldfashioned clothes . . .

It was enough to make her reach for her pen. She wrote, 'A friend is the difference between being happy and unhappy. A friend makes an empty room seem full . . .'

She wrote until the bell rang, and the other students around her filed to the front of the room to leave their papers on the teacher's desk. Cassie hesitated, wondering if her essay was good enough to turn in. Finally, she wrote her name at the top and left it on the top of the pile before hurrying to find her next class.

After the last period, she stood in front of her locker, selecting books to take with her, when she felt someone at her side. Looking up, Cassie was surprised to see her English teacher, Mrs. Blake.

'I read your essay, Cassie,' the teacher said.

Cassie felt a flicker of alarm; was it really terrible? Maybe the teacher wanted to send her to another class.

But Mrs. Blake smiled. 'I think you have a lot of potential. I'm so glad you're in my class this semester. Have you thought of going on to college after you finish high school?'

College? Cassie knew that her face had flushed in surprise. She might as well have dreamed of flying to the moon. 'I can't,' she murmured.

'Why not?' the teacher asked. She seemed genuinely interested.

'I don't have the money; I don't have any money,' Cassie tried to explain. 'My parents – don't believe in schooling.'

'How shortsighted of them,' the teacher replied briskly. 'There are ways, Cassie. Scholarships, if your grades are good enough, student loans, part-time jobs. We'll talk about this later, all right? But don't set your sights too low; you're an intelligent, talented person – remember that.'

Cassie simply blinked in surprise; but when Mrs. Blake walked away, she shut her locker and went to find her bus, still hearing an echo of the teacher's comment. Intelligent, talented ... could it be true? And college – it was a frightening, but exciting thought ... people who went to college were teachers and counselors and even judges . . . they lived in a wider world than her family did.

On the bus, she was so deep in thought that she didn't see Angela until the other girl sat down beside her. 'Still in one piece, are you?'

Cassie nodded. 'It wasn't so bad.'

Angela looked at the big stack of books on Cassie's lap. 'Lord, girl, you trying to graduate next week?'

'I have a lot to catch up on,' Cassie explained, knowing that she sounded defensive. 'Besides, I haven't been able to have books in so long.'

'Why not? Your folks too broke?'

Cassie shook her head. 'My parents don't have a lot, but it's more than that. My dad wouldn't let me go to the library or read books that didn't agree with his opinions. It's as if I've spent most of my life at the bottom of a well, just glimpsing the rest of the world far above, way out of reach. I may be in jail here' – she lowered her voice, glancing around at the rest of the students on the bus, though no one seemed to be paying attention to their conversation –' but in a way, I feel freer than I did at home.'

Angela looked unconvinced. 'You try leaving the school, you won't feel so free.'

Cassie shrugged; it was too hard to explain. 'How was your day?'

'So-so,' Angela told her, but her tone was

unusually mild. 'Got a B on the geometry test. And I think I got a part in the spring play.'

'Really?' Cassie grinned at her roommate. 'Tell me about it.'

When they reached the girls' home, the McNaughten girls climbed off the bus and up the steps to the big building. Another counselor was waiting to usher them inside. Cassie thought of Angela's comment; it was true that their movements seemed to be carefully monitored. But except for missing Seth – and that was a major drawback – this didn't seem such a bad place anymore. Even Angela seemed human enough, once you got past her tough facade.

Cassie dumped her books on her bed, then took her history text and went down to the lounge to find some reference books in the bookcase. She worked for an hour on the history report, until several other girls came in and turned on the TV, switching to music videos. The blaring music sounded strange to Cassie's unaccustomed ears, and she couldn't think. She picked up her books and papers and went back to her room.

Angela was curled up on her bed, apparently asleep. But as Cassie sat down on her own bed, she heard a muffled sob. 'Are you okay?'

'Mind your own business!' came the fierce response. Angela wiped her eyes and frowned, a wrinkled sheet of paper in one hand.

'I just –' Cassie shrugged. 'I just wanted to help, that's all.'

'Can't nobody help.' Angela wadded the paper into a ball and threw it toward the wall. It bounced into a corner. 'My little girl, she got an earache and she cried all night. And I can't be there with her, 'cause I'm stuck in this fool place.'

'Oh, Angela.' Cassie was flooded with sympathy. 'That's awful. Is she okay?'

'I don't know. My mama don't know when she can get her to a doctor – no money left for bus fare. And anyhow, I want to be with her.'

'How old is she, your little girl?'

'Almost two,' Angela said. She took a small framed picture from her bureau drawer and held it out. 'This is my baby, Terri Lynn.'

Cassie moved closer to study the small round face, the bright eyes, and the wide grin. 'Oh, she's adorable. Angela, how come you're here, if you have a baby at home?'

'Missed too much school, and I'd been in trouble before,' Angela said, her tone glum. 'But how could I go to school when I had a baby at home, and she sick half the time, and my mom trying to keep her job and no money for babysitters? But the judge got mad 'cause I yelled at him in court and he stuck me here, so I'd stay in school.'

'What about Terri Lynn's father? Can't he help?'

Angela shook her head. 'Ain't seen him since she was born; he wanted to play, not pay.' Her face crumbled. Cassie put one arm around her roommate, holding her as she sobbed. But this time, instead of Angela's problems, Cassie thought of her own.

This could be her – would soon be her. What would she do with a baby; how could she take care of it alone, without even her parents' help? No matter what the teacher said, college was still an impossible dream. Angela couldn't even stay in high school until she was forced. How could Cassie possibly manage the time and money for college, with a baby to take care of?

The excitement of her first day at school faded as reality returned. Cassie felt as if she had traded one prison for another. This time it was not her father who held her back, but her own body, with the baby forming inside.

Why hadn't they been more careful? Why hadn't they waited to have sex?

Oh, Seth, Cassie thought, but this time with more anger than yearning. Seth, maybe love isn't enough.

Chapter 8

Dear Cassie,

I'm still stuck here, waiting for the truck to be fixed. I walked up to the interstate and tried to hitch a ride, but no one would pick me up.

Every hour that passes seems to pull you further away from me; I feel like such a failure. I've let you down. But I won't give up. I am coming, Cassie. I'll get there, I swear it. I won't be like my dad, I won't. I'll be there when you need me, Cassie.

I love you.
Seth

Seth scribbled the lines on the yellow sheet of paper, then pushed it back into his pocket. After trying unsuccessfully to hitch a ride, he'd finally walked back to the service station when night fell. Ollie Rockford, sitting patiently in his truck, had shared a bologna sandwich with him and bought him a Coke from the machine.

Seth, the gun heavy in his jacket pocket, had

felt guilty for accepting the gifts. But his stomach was so hollow that it made his knees weak, and his mouth watered when he looked at the thick-cut, homemade sandwich.

'Thanks,' he'd muttered and gulped it down, ignoring the dog's accusing stare. The food had hardly taken the edge off his hunger. Seth drank the canned soda more slowly, trying to fill up his stomach with liquid, fool it into thinking he'd had more to eat during this long day.

Then he'd curled up in the back of the truck with a blanket that smelled of dog, while Ollie stretched out across the seat of the cab, his jacket over him, with the dog for a pillow. The lady inside the service station had closed up and gone home long ago.

The night seemed to stretch on forever. Seth turned and twisted on the hard surface of the truck bed, the blanket soon damp with spring dew and offering little warmth. He almost envied Ollie the body warmth of the big dog, though Bobo would never have allowed Seth to get that close.

Seth looked up at the stars hanging low in the clear black sky and thought about Cassie. Was she thinking about him? Or was she asleep now in some featureless dormitory? He sighed when he thought of Cassie sleeping, remembering how soft her skin was. She'd rested in his arms as he'd touched her cheek, her neck, and then

. . . He felt such longing that he had to push those memories aside.

What kind of place was this girls' home, anyhow? But it didn't matter; he would get there, somehow, and he would take Cassie away. They would find a way to be together, a place where they could share those dreams they'd talked about back in the community center, or upstairs in his apartment bedroom. Cassie's eyes had shone when they talked of a future together. There had to be a way, and Seth would find it.

He would be responsible; he had to, he was going to be a father. He would be a better father than his own, the man he barely remembered. He would hold the baby with loving hands, he'd change those stinky diapers, even. He wouldn't yell and make the baby cry; most of all, he wouldn't leave. And he and Cassie would smile down on the baby, together.

The baby was becoming real to him, now. Seth could almost see it, a little guy with Cassie's hazel eyes and maybe Seth's broad forehead. This baby wouldn't have to know how it felt to be alone, to be afraid, to have to be the man of the family when you were too young to even know what that meant. Seth would take care of them all, one way or another.

The image of this bright future, even if he couldn't quite see the details, how he would manage all this, lulled him closer to sleep.

Relaxing, Seth's eyelids drooped and he slipped toward sleep, despite the hard surface beneath him, the chilly air all around.

Then he remembered that Cassie had talked about giving the baby up, and his pulse raced. His whole body stiffened, and he was wide awake at once, rigid with fear.

Don't, Cassie, he thought now, wishing he could call her, see her. Oh, God, would he ever make it to Knoxville and to Cassie? He wasn't sure if it was a prayer or a cry of desperation that rose in his mind. He had to get to her in time. 'Don't give up our baby, my baby, Cassie,' he murmured.

Staring into the dark sky, even the twinkling stars seemed colder, unfeeling. He might lose not only Cassie but his baby, and no one seemed to care.

It seemed an eternity before dawn streaked the sky with fingers of color. The rumbling of traffic on the interstate increased, and Seth rubbed his tired eyes. He'd managed little sleep.

He stretched and sat up, rubbing his sore arms; he could feel the imprint of the hard truck bed all over his body.

The sound of a car made him look around hopefully. It wasn't the truck parts arriving, nor even the woman to open the tiny station. Seth stared at the faded green station wagon with specks of rust on its doors. The woman behind the wheel drove it slowly, and he saw that one of the tires was very low.

She pulled the wagon up in front of the dark station; there was just light enough to see the driver's worried expression.

Seth twisted to peer through the back window of the pickup truck. Ollie was still asleep, his baseball cap pulled over his face to block the light. The dog lifted its ears when it saw Seth, but otherwise didn't move.

The woman opened the car door and got out, staring at the front left-hand tire and shaking her head.

Seth got out of the truck and walked over.

'Do you work here? Is the station open yet?' the driver asked. She was in her midtwenties, he guessed, and her blond hair was pushed back from her face, which was pretty enough but drawn now with lines of worry.

Seth shook his head. 'We're waiting for a part for the truck; the station won't open till seven,' he told her. He'd read the sign on the door and, anyhow, Ollie had talked to the manager about when the supply truck would arrive with his parts.

She shook her head. Inside the car, Seth saw a baby strapped into a safety seat. The sleepy-eyed child made him swallow hard; it looked too much like the baby face he'd been drawing in his imagination.

'Maybe if you put some air in,' he suggested. 'I don't know how.' She looked at him uncertainly.

'Pull it over to the air hose,' he told her. His mom's old car was always needing something done; Seth knew all the basic stuff.

But when he bent with the hose in hand, he touched the worn treads of the tire and shook his head. 'It won't do any good. See this – you've got a nail in the tire. It needs a patch, and those will be locked up inside the station.'

The woman looked worried, and the baby inside the car wailed softly. She hurried to unstrap the infant and cradle it against her. She held the baby carefully, murmuring soothing words.

The baby quieted. Watching her made Seth feel better inside, too, though he didn't know why.

'You got a spare?' he asked.

She nodded. 'In the back.'

'How about a jack?'

She made a face. 'I don't know.'

'Open it up and I'll check,' Seth offered. He pulled the spare tire out and found the jack in the well beneath. Putting it together, he jacked up the car, removed the lug nuts, and pulled off the tire. The driver took a bottle of juice from a diaper bag and gave it to the baby, then she walked up and down, soothing the child and watching over his shoulder.

When Seth had the spare in place and had put the damaged tire in the back of the wagon, he let the car down carefully, took apart the jack, and put it back, too.

'How far are you going?' Seth asked her. 'Just to Cookeville; I had to spend the night with my mom, out in the country. She's had pneumonia, and my husband's working the night shift,' the woman told him, sighing. She held out a five-dollar bill. 'I appreciate your help. I wish I had more to give you.'

Seth flushed; he wished he could wave the money away. But he might need it; he'd spent his last dime on the phone call to Cassie. 'Thanks,' he said.

Then, as she strapped the baby back inside, he had a thought. 'Hey, would you mind giving me a ride into Cookeville?'

She looked at him in surprise. 'I thought you were waiting for a part for your truck.'

'My granddad is,' Seth lied earnestly. 'But if I wait for the part to get here, I'll be late to school. Could you just take me into town?'

'Sure,' she told him.

Seth ran across the lot to the truck, thankful that it was far enough away so that the woman wouldn't hear if he spoke softly. 'I got another ride. Thanks for your help, Ollie.'

The old man rubbed his eyes like a kid and

sat up stiffly. 'That's okay. Take care of yourself, sonny.'

Seth felt his spirits lift. He was moving again, he had a little money, and he hadn't stolen it, either.

I'm on my way, Cassie, he thought as the blond-haired woman pulled the car back onto the interstate. She drove slowly, and they reached Cookeville just as morning traffic thickened on the roadways. She pulled off the interstate at the second exit.

'I'll take you on home, if you like,' she offered. 'Or to your high school. Which side of town are you on?'

'That's okay,' Seth told her. 'I can catch a bus; just drop me off here.'

He waved at her before she pulled back onto the highway, then walked into the doughnut shop on the corner of the strip of stores.

He hadn't meant to spend any of his money, but his stomach growled when he walked inside. Fingering the folded bill in his pocket, Seth stared into the glass case. Finally, he bought a thick sweetroll and a small carton of milk, too hungry to resist the sugary, greasy smells. He could have eaten a dozen doughnuts, but he needed his money for a bus ticket.

'Where's the bus station?' he asked the woman behind the counter. 'How much is a ticket to Knoxville, you think?'

She mentioned a street name, not looking up as she wiped the smooth surface with a damp cloth. 'To Knoxville, I don't know, ten, fifteen dollars, maybe.'

Seth felt a sinking feeling. He still didn't have enough money for a ticket. Now what?

He walked out of the doughnut shop and looked around. The parklng lot was crowded with cars, and the street was filled with early morning traffic.

Could he get another ride? But he remembered his futile attempts at hitchhiking, and he didn't have any more time to waste. He should have been in Knoxville days ago; Cassie was waiting. Worse, she might be signing away the baby right now; maybe they were hassling her, giving her a hard time. Seth wasn't sure who 'they' would be, but he had an image of shadowy, sinister figures, with Cassie under their control.

He had to get to Knoxville.

As he stared out at the cars and trucks that zoomed past on the main road, Seth turned over ideas in his mind, trying to find a way.

A blue car backed out of the parking lot, and a small red sports car pulled into the empty space. It was a convertible, and the top was down. But the man behind the wheel took the key from the ignition and slipped it in his pocket as he walked into the doughnut shop.

Seth didn't know how to hot-wire a car, and besides, the car was in easy view from the shop's window.

Another car pulled away, and this time a yellow cab drove into the resulting space. The driver, a short man in a blue windbreaker, got out and walked into the shop.

Seth stared at the taxi, his mind whirling with thoughts. How could he get to Cassie, with no money, and no more time to waste?

The minutes stretched slowly, then the taxi driver came out, a cup of coffee in one hand, a chocolate doughnut in the other. He put the doughnut into his mouth and opened the front door.

Seth ran up to the cab. 'Hey, I need a ride.' The driver took the pastry out of his mouth, swallowing. 'I'm off-duty, kid.'

'Come on, just to the bus station.'

The cabdriver stared at him, his expression suspicious. 'You got money, kid?'

'Sure, I do.' Seth reached into his jeans pocket, pulled out the wadded-up dollar bills that were left from the five he'd gotten for changing the flat. He waved the bills quickly, before the driver could see exactly how much money Seth held, then shoved them back into his jeans pocket.

'Okay, it's on my way. Climb in,' the man said.

Seth opened the back door and got in, sliding

over the worn seat, his heart racing.

The driver put his steaming coffee into a mug holder on the door, stuffed more doughnut into his mouth, and put the key into the ignition. 'Got a fare to the bus station,' he mumbled into the mike hanging from the bottom of his dash. A burst of static answered him.

Seth blinked; he hadn't thought about the twoway radio. That might screw up his whole plan. But it was too late to back out now.

They rode toward the center of town, past college buildings and small stores, a car lot, a church.

The driver finished his doughnut and sipped the hot coffee. He didn't ask any questions, and Seth was thankful; he was too nervous to make up any more stories.

The streets rolled by; a red light stopped them, then another. A truck ahead of them backfired, and Seth jumped.

Finally, Seth saw the bus station ahead. The cabdriver put on his turn signal and braked for the turn. Seth leaned forward from the back-seat.

'Don't stop,' he said.

'What? There's the station, kid; I'll drop you in the front.'

'Don't stop, you hear me? And turn off the radio.'

'What –' The taxi driver twisted to peer at

Seth over the seat. His eyes widened when he saw the gun Seth had pulled from his jacket pocket.

'Keep driving,' Seth said.

Chapter 9

Dear Diary,

I didn't know that Angela had a baby, too. No wonder she's hard to live with, sometimes. How awful not to have your little girl with you – she must miss her baby so much.

What will happen to my baby when it's born? I need to ask the counselor, but I keep losing my nerve; I'm afraid to hear the answer.

I wish we'd done this all differently. Oh, Seth, I wish we'd thought about it before we made love. We didn't think about consequences.

'Yo, Cassie,' Angela called. 'The dragon lady wants you down in the sessions room. Come on and get your head shrunk with the rest of us.'

Cassie put down her pencil with a sigh. She slipped her diary under her pillow, then followed Angela down to the group counseling session. Cassie sat down in an empty chair; as the counselor and then the other girls talked, Cassie listened and said little. She discovered that many of the girls had problems at home: parents who beat them, parents on drugs, parents who drank too much, parents who were never home.

Stella's mom had gone off for five days, leaving her home to take care of four younger brothers and sisters.

'And I didn't have any money to buy food, and there was nothing in the cabinets, and the milk was gone. My baby brother was crying, and I didn't know what to do; Mom told me not to tell anyone she wasn't home . . .' Stella's voice wobbled, and she sobbed at the memory.

Cassie felt her own eyes dampen out of sympathy.

'How did you feel?' Mrs. Porter asked. The counselor's voice was kind.

'I was so scared. They were begging me for something to eat, and I didn't have anything to give them, and I thought, what if the baby dies . . .' Stella cried harder.

The girl sitting next to her patted Stella on the shoulder and handed her a tissue from the box on the table.

The counselor asked, 'Were you angry at your mother?'

'No, she didn't mean to stay away so long. If she hadn't been drinking, she wouldn't have done it. She forgets everything when she drinks . . . I know she loves us, really, she does,' Stella insisted, wiping her cheeks with the tissue.

'Is that how a loving mother acts?' Mrs. Porter asked quietly. 'Leaving her children alone, without food in the house or anyone to call in case of emergency?'

Stella looked stubborn. 'I know she loves me,' she said. 'I just want to go home. I know she'll do better this time.'

When the session ended, Cassie went back to her room alone, thinking. As harsh as her father had sometimes been, at least Cassie had always had food to eat, always had someone at home to look to for help.

Until her dad kicked her out. She sighed at the thought. Her father had always said that he loved her, that he did what he did for the good of the children. At some point, she had stopped quite believing that, yet it was hard to abandon faith in your parents completely. When did love become something else? When did you stop looking out for your child and begin looking out for yourself, protecting your own beliefs, your own life at the expense of your child?

And was it love to keep a baby when you weren't ready to take care of it? Cassie opened the door to her bedroom; it was empty. Angela was out of the room, but she had left a catalogue open on her bed; she had brought it up earlier from the pile of junk mail in the lounge.

The sales flyer had been turned to a page of

colorful nursery furniture. Cassie stood over the bed and admired the picture. The room in the photo was filled with white furniture and bright linens, stuffed animals in a rocking chair, pictures on the wall, a lamp with a teddy bear stand.

If you could bring a baby home to a room like that . . . if you could bring a baby home, at all. Cassie didn't have a home. What would happen to the baby after it was born?

The counselor had mentioned adoption. Was there a husband and wife waiting somewhere, a couple who had a nursery all fixed up, bright and inviting, ready for a baby? A couple with a home and a backyard with room for swing sets and tricycles, a couple who were married and stable, with steady jobs and the serenity to offer a baby love without reservations?

She had so little to offer her baby compared to that. How could it be love to hold on to an infant when you had nothing to give it? Yet, what would Seth say about giving up the baby? He'd sounded alarmed on the phone when she mentioned the possibility. But wouldn't he want the best for their baby, too?

Cassie took a deep breath; she'd talk to the counselor tomorrow about giving up the baby to a better home. Then, feeling a weight lift, she lay down across her bed. The pregnancy left her more tired than usual, and the stress of her first day at school had been enormous. Her eyes slowly shut.

Angela woke her, banging into the room with her usual careless energy. 'Hey, sleepyhead. It's early. Come down to the lounge; we're watching the new music videos. This new band is hot.'

'Okay,' Cassie said sleepily. She didn't really want to leave the comfort of her bed, but she hated to brush aside any friendly overture from her unpredictable roommate.

She rubbed her eyes, gathering the energy to sit up, then frowned. A strange feeling in her stomach made her pause; was it indigestion?

But the faint impulse came again, the tiniest brush of movement, like a butterfly caught in a jar. Cassie's eyes opened wide, and she put one hand to her stomach.

'Angela!'

'What – you sick?' Angela stopped to stare at her. 'If you got to throw up, get the trash can, quick; don't mess up the room.'

'I think I felt the baby!' Cassie felt goose bumps rise on her arms, she almost didn't believe it. It was moving. He was moving, or she. The baby was real, her baby, Seth's baby. For the first time, she could picture it, imagine holding the baby in her arms, kissing the smooth forehead, counting the tiny pink fingers and toes.

'Oh, let me feel,' Angela said. She hurried

across the room to lean over the bed and touch Cassie's abdomen lightly. For a moment, she concentrated. 'Wow, go, kid!'

It came again, the touch of butterfly wings. Cassie forgot everything outside her to concentrate within, on the new life growing there. I love you, little one, she thought with a sudden fierce rush of emotion. You're part of me, and part of Seth. What could be more precious than a bit of both of us together, a sign of our love for each other?

How could she think of giving up her baby?

Angela put out a hand to pull her up. 'Lucky you,' she said wistfully. 'But just wait. I remember before Terri Lynn was born – I thought sure she'd be a boy – kicked me like a pro linebacker, she did. And when I complained, my momma said, easier in than out. Wait till you have the screaming in the middle of the night, and diapers to change, and bottles to wash, ain't so easy, then.'

Cassie was barely listening. She followed Angela down to the lounge where the TV blared, still with her senses turned inward, delighting at each flicker of movement.

They found seats on the long couch as the other girls scooted over to make room. Cassie tried to watch the television; the bright screen was still a novelty to her. The music videos were loud; sometimes the tunes sounded like so much noise, but the softer melodies, the ones that sang of love, reminded her painfully of Seth.

Seth didn't know she had felt the baby. Cassie wished Seth could put his hand over her belly as Angela had done and share the tiny movements. Seth was missing so much. Would they let him in to see her, if he ever made it to Knoxville? Poor Seth, was he still stuck with a broken-down truck? She felt guilty for being so intent on her first day at school, her own worries, that she hadn't thought of him much today. Seth, I hope you're okay, she tried to tell him silently.

When ten o'clock came, one of the girls changed the channel.

'Hey, put it back,' another complained.

'I have to see the news,' the first girl told them. 'I have a current events quiz tomorrow.'

Despite the grumbles, they all sat and watched the somber headlines. Cassie's attention drifted; she put one hand quietly over her stomach and waited for the baby to make its presence known again.

But after European trade talks and a train wreck in Iowa, the newscaster said, 'And the teenaged boy who allegedly hijacked a taxicab and its driver in Cookeville is still being sought. State police reported –'

Cassie sat up straighter, wishing she'd been paying closer attention. It couldn't be Seth, could it? He wouldn't do anything like that. But hadn't he been outside of Cookeville when he last spoke to her? And he'd sounded so desperate. She listened to the short news story anxiously.

'Police have traced the cab's movements up to Interstate 40; the taxi is believed to be headed east, toward Knoxville.'

I'll get to Knoxville somehow, Seth had said. The baby moved inside her, but this time, Cassie didn't smile. Oh, Seth, she thought. What have you done?

Chapter 10

Cassie,
Please don't hate me. I had to do it.

He couldn't add that to his letter, not now. Seth gripped the gun hard and pushed the thought away.

'What's this, a joke? I ain't laughing,' the cab-driver said. But his voice sounded strained.

'It's no joke; I mean it,' Seth said sharply. 'And this is not a toy. Now, turn off the radio and keep your eyes on the road.'

He didn't want the driver to look too hard at the gun; he might see that the chambers were empty. The man turned his head back toward the front of the cab.

'Hey, I only got a few dollars – everybody uses credit cards now to pay, you know. You can have my wallet; just don't get crazy with the gun, okay?'

'I don't want your money; turn off the radio,' Seth ordered, his tone sharp.

The driver leaned forward and clicked a switch on the dash-mounted mike, and Seth relaxed just a little. The static and snatches of jumbled conversation died, and silence filled the cab.

'Go back to the interstate,' Seth told the man.

'What do you want, kid?' the driver asked him, glancing back over his shoulder. 'What are you going to do with a stolen cab? It's not exactly easy to hide, you know.'

'I don't want your cab,' Seth said.

They followed a steady line of traffic, inching along the main road. A traffic light flashed red, and the cab stopped. Seth kept his left hand over the gun, trying to shield it from any inquisitive eyes in the neighboring traffic lanes.

Then he inhaled sharply, his shoulders tensing again as he spotted a police car sitting just off the intersection.

The cabdriver had seen it, too. His shoulders stiffened and he almost turned the wheel; Seth saw the small motion.

Seth lifted the gun and pressed it to the back of the driver's neck. He saw the man flinch from the touch of the steel barrel.

'Don't even think about it. Just keep driving; no sudden moves.'

It was the longest red light Seth had ever seen. Finally, it faded, and the green light appeared. Traffic moved slowly, and the cab rolled forward again.

They inched along the city streets; Seth hadn't thought Cookeville could go on for so long. Every car and, worse, every truck looming over them in the congested lanes held the possibility of someone spotting the gun. He tried to keep it covered with his hand, tried to watch all around, tried to keep the driver always under his eye.

Would they never reach the interstate? Finally, they crossed one last intersection, and Seth saw the signs. INTERSTATE 40 EAST. 'Turn there!'

The cab pulled into the access lane and back onto the interstate. As the vehicle surged forward into the faster traffic, Seth breathed a little easier.

The driver glanced at him in the rearview mirror. 'If you don't want the cab, why are you doing this? This is not some stupid prank, is it?'

Seth would have laughed, but his throat was too tight. 'No, it's no joke; I told you before.'

'Then why? You're not high or anything, are you? You know that stuffs not good for you.'

Again, Seth wanted to laugh, with more hysteria than humor. 'No,' he said. 'I'm not high, I'm not drunk. I'm just desperate. Look, you drive, don't speed, don't attract attention. I just want to get to Knoxville, then you can go home and take your cab with you. I don't want anyone to get hurt, so just do what I say, okay?'

The driver's expression was puzzled. 'Why do you want to get to Knoxville so bad?'

Seth thought of Cassie, Cassie locked away in the girls' home, Cassie carrying his baby. 'None of your business,' he said.

The cab settled into a steady speed, and some of Seth's tension lessened. But with the drone of the wheels against the pavement, the soft roar of the engine, his sleepless night began to pull at his eyelids, making them droop, making the gun heavier and heavier in his hand.

The passing landscape, trees and fields and more trees rising steadily toward the mountains, blurred. Seth's eyes blinked shut.

He jerked them open. If he went to sleep, dropped the gun, the driver would take advantage of his weakness. Seth would never make it to Knoxville, and Cassie would think he didn't care enough to come after her. And the baby – what would happen to the baby?

He gripped the gun so tightly that his fingers felt numb. Seth changed hands for a moment, flexing his fingers. He looked up into the rearview mirror; the driver shifted his eyes back toward the road, but he had been watching.

'Talk to me,' Seth said. He had to stay awake. 'Talk? What about? We ain't exactly the best of friends, kid,' the cabdriver said. 'You hold me up at gunpoint and take me off to kingdom come, and now you want to have a nice chat?' His fear seemed to have faded; his voice was angry, a quiet smoldering anger that could flare up at any moment like an almost-extinguished blaze.

Seth felt the danger in the man, and his nerves tightened. 'Never mind.'

He looked around as a big eighteen-wheeler pulled into the next lane, passing them. Seth put one arm over the gun, trying to hide it, and stared up at the cab. He saw the truck driver reach forward and pick up the mike of his radio.

Seth felt the hair on his neck rise. Coincidence? Or something more?

The truck pulled ahead of them, but Seth felt new apprehension. He looked at the clock on the dash; it was almost noon. 'Turn on the radio.'

The cabdriver's thick brows pulled together; he frowned at Seth in the mirror. 'You said –'

'Not the two-way radio; I want to hear the news.'

The driver hesitated, then slowly leaned forward and turned a knob.

A country song blared abruptly from the speakers, then slowed to a twangy end. Seth listened to a commercial for a tire company, then two people selling sofas. Finally, the announcer came on with the twelve o'clock news.

'In Nashville, the governor signed a bill today raising some state taxes, despite objections from consumer groups . . .'

Seth took a deep breath. Maybe he was worring for nothing. But the announcer's next sentence made him sit up straight, feeling as if he'd been struck by an electric current.

'The cab alleged to have been hijacked in Cookeville this morning was spotted earlier heading east on Interstate 40. State troopers are on the lookout for the stolen taxi. Stay tuned for further developments. And now, the weather, after a message from the Sporting Goods Shop.'

Seth ignored the rest of the commercial jingle. He sat rigid with anger, breathing quickly. If the state police found him, spotted the taxi – they wouldn't be afraid of one small gun, and he had no bullets.

Seth glared at the driver, at the back of his head where his neck was reddened from too much sun, at the side of his face as the driver stared straight ahead at the pavement in front of the speeding taxi. His expression was noncommittal, except that his lips were pressed together tightly. And his hands gripped the steering wheel so hard that his knuckles were white.

'What'd you do?' Seth demanded. 'How did they find out so fast?'

'I didn't do anything,' the driver muttered. But this time he avoided Seth's eyes in the mirror.

Something was wrong; how did the police know the cab was being hijacked? And how did they know so fast in which direction it had been taken?

He'd turned off the two-way radio, first thing. Seth stared at the radio attached to the lower part of the dash, and this time he saw something he'd missed before – a tiny red light on the console.

'It's still on! I told you to turn that thing off, and you tricked me!' Seth almost yelled. He lifted the gun, pressed it harder against the back of the man's neck. 'Turn it off, all of it, not just the incoming messages.'

'It doesn't matter; we're out of range, now,' the driver said. But he leaned forward and pushed another switch, and the red light died.

But it was too late, now. Seth thought furiously. 'All that talk about where we were going – about the gun – you just wanted to let them know, didn't you? I should shoot you right now.'

He saw the driver swallow hard. Served him right, Seth thought angrily. The driver didn't know Seth couldn't shoot anyone with an empty gun; let him worry.

But what should Seth do now? Get off the interstate, for a start. The police would be looking for him, looking for the cab. And its bright yellow paint wasn't exactly hard to spot.

Seth looked at the road signs; he was tantalizingly closer to Knoxville. He considered just going on, trying to make it to the city, to find Cassie. But he looked ahead and saw a car with flashing lights. His heart leapt inside his chest; he thought he couldn't breathe.

The driver had spotted it, too. But the momentary flash of hope in the driver's expression faded, and his shoulders sagged.

A second later Seth also recognized that it was a signal car preceding an extra-wide trailer, not a police car. But the state troopers could be over the next hill. He had to get off the interstate, try to find a different route.

'Take the next exit,' Seth ordered, his tone grim. He didn't trust the taxi driver an inch, and he was still filled with anger.

The driver grunted, but he turned onto the next exit, pulling off the highway onto a small road that led up toward the mountains.

Seth tried to remember the name of the road from the map Ollie had given him, but it didn't stir his memory, and he couldn't pull the map out now to study it. He could tell by the tension in the driver's shoulders that he was considering making a move.

'Don't think about it,' Seth told him. 'I'm too mad at you right now; don't tempt me.'

The taxi chugged up the small road until the interstate was out of sight behind a clump of trees. Seth looked at the gas tank; it was still half full.

'Pull over here,' he said.

When the vehicle came to a slow stop, as if the driver didn't want to release even a tenuous control, Seth lifted the gun. 'Get out,' he said.

The driver bit his lip, then reached into his jeans pocket.

Seth tensed. He leaned forward over the seat back that separated them, holding the gun closer to the driver.

'I'm just getting out my wallet,' the driver said, glancing back at him. 'Look, I got a few dollars; you can have them, okay?'

'I don't want your money, I told you,' Seth said. 'I'm not a crook. I just needed to get to Knoxville, that's all I wanted. You had to make it hard.'

The driver's face had paled; he watched the gun, then glanced at Seth's face, then back to the gun.

The gun had no bullets, but it was hard metal. The man wasn't expecting a blow – if Seth caught him on the side of the head, it might knock him out, keep him from reporting the theft of the taxi right away, buy Seth some necessary time.

And it might kill him. Seth remembered the

boy in junior high who'd been struck in the head by a baseball and died almost instantly. Could Seth take the chance? While he debated, and the driver sat as if afraid to move, a thin sheen of sweat coating his face, Seth glanced at the wallet the driver had left lying open on the seat.

He saw photos of two small children. Open, grinning faces: a girl and a boy. Some of Seth's anger retreated. 'Those your kids?' he asked unwillingly.

The driver nodded quickly. 'That's my girl, Sara,' he said. 'She's in first grade. And Matt, my boy, he's got a ball game after school today. I told him I'd be there. I even changed shifts so I could go and watch. He'll be waiting for me, you know?'

Something in Seth softened, despite his frustrations. A little boy was waiting for his father. And if that father never came home? He couldn't do it.

The knowledge made his voice grim, knowing the extra risk he was taking. 'Get out, slowly,' he told the cabdriver. 'Take the keys.'

The man gulped visibly, then opened his door. Holding the gun on his hostage, Seth opened his own door and slipped carefully out. He motioned the man to the rear of the cab.

The driver obeyed, now looking puzzled. 'Open the trunk,' Seth told him.

'You're not going to put me in there?' The man's voice flared with panic. 'A person could suffocate.'

'Open the trunk,' Seth repeated, trying not to see the raw fear in the driver's eyes.

The driver inserted the key slowly into the trunk and swung up the lid.

'Step back,' Seth told him. 'Stop right there.' Keeping the cabdriver in his peripheral vision, Seth made a quick sweep through the trunk. There – a piece of tough twine. Would it do?

He picked up the rope and, motioning with the gun, directed the driver to the nearest good-sized tree, a tough young maple.

'If you struggle, I'm going to knock you out,' Seth warned. The driver seemed so relieved not to be locked into the trunk, he made no protest as Seth had him hug the tree, then tied his hands securely on the other side.

Maybe that would hold him for a few hours, Seth thought, inspecting the driver with his arms around the tree trunk. Maybe he wouldn't make it to his son's ball game, but he should be home by nightfall; that twine wouldn't take too much pulling before it shredded. What it would do to the driver's wrists, Seth tried not to think about, nor how forlorn the man looked, alone in the clearing beside the little road.

Seth turned his back resolutely and hurried back to the cab. Taking the key from the trunk, he slid behind the steering wheel and started the engine. He backed into the road, then tried to decide what to do.

Everything inside him pulled him toward Knoxville, and the straightest path was the interstate. But that's where the police would be watching for him, and the cab would stand out like a sore thumb. That would be too stupid.

Seth turned the cab away from the interstate, toward the small road that wound up into the mountains. He'd have to find another route.

'I'm on my way, Cassie,' he said.

Chapter 11

Dear Diary,

Is Seth the one who hijacked the taxi? I keep telling myself that it can't be true, it must be someone else. But I remember his voice, how desperate he sounded, and I just know he's the one the police are after. It makes me sick to think about him doing something illegal – he's going to be in so much trouble. And he did it because of me. I feel guilty; I should have told him not to do it. But how could I, when I never thought he'd do something so crazy? I don't know what to think, but I'm so afraid. He'll never make it to Knoxville, now, not with the police after him. Will I ever see Seth again?

She lay in her bed, sleeping only in snatches, worrying about Seth. Fatigue pulled at her eyelids, but every time Cassie drowsed, there were images ready to haunt her.

So she stared into the darkness and thought about the afternoon Seth had had the asthma attack, how he had wheezed and coughed and turned pale, and how frightened she had been that he would Stop breathing, die. He'd gotten some relief from his inhaler, then she'd urged him to go home and rest. She was afraid to leave him alone – what if he had another attack while he walked home? – so for the first time, she had gone back to his apartment.

They expected his mother to be there, but instead they found a note: Marla had been called in to the restaurant to do an extra shift for another waitress who'd gone home sick.

Making love had been the last thing on their minds. She only wanted to make sure he was okay, that he wouldn't choke to death, suffocated as he fought with his own body to breathe. Seth, despite his physical distress, was obviously embarrassed by the littered apartment with its stale smoky air, and between his wheezing tried to apologize for the mess.

Cassie waved that aside and urged him to lie down. She brought him a glass of water and sat beside the bed, holding his hand and waiting till his breathing returned to normal. And when he could breathe again without struggling, when his chest rose and fell with a more normal rhythm, Cassie was suddenly aware of the silent apartment around them; she realized they'd never been alone before.

And his grip on her hand tightened. She

looked down at Seth and saw so much love and so much longing in his eyes that she didn't think what it might lead to; she bent down and kissed him gently. He put his arms around her, and somehow she was lying beside him in the rumpled bed.

That was the day she discovered what love between a man and a woman could be. No one had ever explained sex to her, and she hadn't been prepared for the sweetness of his touch, nor how her own body would respond so urgently.

Her father talked constantly about sin, *sin*, which was so horrible, so wrapped up with hellfire and damnation. Cassie had always thought sin would be easy to spot, draped in the worldly excesses her father shouted about in his long prayer sessions at home. Sin would be a hideous monster, dark and ugly and frightening.

Sharing love with Seth had been a series of surprises, each bringing them closer in body and in spirit. Even though Seth had never had sex before, either, and they had awkward moments, clumsy and even a little painful, Cassie had felt his love surround her, lift her past the unknown. Being one with the person you loved – shouldn't it be a holy thing, a beautiful, uplifting moment of light?

Her father started suspecting she was Seeing a boy. She felt guilt about that afternoon, yet the pleasure they had found together was also hard to forget, the increasing understanding between them, the urgency of their passion, the sweetness of silent communion as they lay close together afterward, while Cassie marveled at how at home she felt in Seth's arms.

Then her father came to the community center to pick her up and saw her walk inside, holding hands with Seth. He would have condemned any boy, Cassie thought bitterly, not just Seth. Her father had sharply limited her time out. After that she saw Seth only momentarily in the supermarket aisles or on the street corner. But her father followed her one day and saw them talking. Then Cassie was restricted to her own home for the long weeks and months that followed. And while she waited for the slow weeks to pass, Cassie first suspected that she might be pregnant.

Now she looked back at all those afternoons had brought – the hearing, her exile, the girls' home, Seth's panic and illegal actions – and, most of all, a baby with no home to welcome it, parents unprepared to support it. So despite the fact that she still refused to call her first knowledge of love a sin, she thought now, alone in the darkness, listening to Angela's uneven breathing, that she and Seth should have waited, they should have thought ahead. The love might be genuine, but the time was wrong.

Cassie turned restlessly on her narrow bed. If they had been older, if they had made a home together, if one or both had a job, if they'd stood up side by side amid flowers and family and friends and proclaimed their commitment to each other, sharing rings and kisses, blessed by God and their community – it would have been so different. Then she wouldn't have had to face the terrible ordeal ahead of her, wrestling with the idea that her baby would be better off without her.

And thinking about surrendering the baby that would be born of her body, the product of that unplanned love, she wept, bitter tears that seeped silently down her cheeks and dampened the pillow. Oh, my baby, my baby, Cassie thought. How can I give you up? She had a terrible premonition that the decision would only get harder, the more the infant grew inside her.

She cried for a long time, silently into her pillow so as not to wake Angela, wanting no questions, no comments.

But once she thought she heard soft sobs across the room, as if her muffled weeping had produced an echo. Cassie lifted her head, frowning into the darkness. But the room was quiet again, maybe she'd imagined it. She pulled the sheet up to her chin and tried to sleep.

When her eyes finally closed, Cassie dreamed

of Seth, Seth holding out his arms to her. The sight of him filled an empty place inside her, and she ran forward eagerly to touch him, to feel his arms around her. She wanted Seth to make her feel safe again, to feel loved. But then it wasn't Seth at all, it was her father, his large powerful hand uplifted, his face angry, his voice booming at her, and she cried out in terror.

Cassie woke abruptly, her heart beating fast. It was only a dream, she told herself, a dream. Pa's not here; he can't hurt me. Not more than he already has, anyhow. She shut her eyes again, but the sleep wouldn't return. That was why she heard the faint movement when Angela slipped out of her bed and tiptoed to the bureau.

Was she up already? It wasn't even daylight, yet. Cassie squinted to see in the faint glimmer of light that seeped beneath their closed door from the night-light in the hall.

Angela was pulling clothes out of her bureau, stuffing them into a bag, no, into her big purse. What was going on?

Was she running away? The big doors downstairs were locked, and the building had a security alarm that would bring the counselors running. Angela had explained all this to Cassie herself, when the two girls first began talking.

Cassie lay with her eyes half closed, pretending to sleep, while she tried to figure out what was happening.

Angela got back into her bed, but she lay stiffly. Cassie didn't think she was asleep. Whatever was happening, it was obviously something Angela didn't want her roommate to know.

Cassie sighed and stared at the mottled ceiling. Finally, she heard the droning of the alarm clock and reached across to shut it off.

Angela sat up, too. Her eyes looked puffy, her cheeks swollen. It was a reflection of the face that Cassie knew she would see when she looked into the mirror, just darker of skin. She'd been right after all; Angela, too, had cried last night.

'You okay?' Cassie asked.

Angela wouldn't meet her eyes. 'Sure, why not?' she mumbled.

Cassie picked up her clothes and headed for the bathroom to shower. She couldn't force the other girl to talk to her, but she knew something was wrong.

As she washed her face, Cassie stared at her own reflection. Her eyelids were swollen, too, her cheeks still flushed. She wished again for some of the makeup that Angela would use to cover the signs of her tears. Was she worried about her little girl? Had she received another letter from her mother?

Cassie took a quick shower, then dried herself, wrapped up in the big towel, and stepped out of the shower stall. She glanced at Angela, who was applying makeup before the steamed-up mirror. Sure enough, the dark-skinned girl had covered up most of the signs of her grief.

'What you staring at?' Angela demanded.

'Wishing I had some makeup, too,' Cassie admitted.

'Why don't you?'

'My father would never let me wear any,' Cassie explained. 'He said women who painted their faces were –' She stopped abruptly, not wanting to insult Angela.

Angela grimaced. 'No man tell me what to wear on my own face. Matter of fact, you'd look better with some color on you – you look like a ghost. Here, try this one.' She held out a tube of bright red lipstick.

Cassie took the metal tube gingerly, as if it might burn her hands. Hellfire and damnation, the echoes in her mind said. But she was fascinated with the bright lipstick and dabbed it on her lips in quick, awkward movements.

'Lord, girl, don't smear it over your face; you look like a clown.' Grinning for the first time that morning, Angela took back the tube. 'Here, wipe that off.'

With a tissue, Cassie removed what she could, then Angela showed her how to follow the outlines of her lips. When the other girl stepped back, Cassie stared at herself in the mirror. Her lips were now a dark crimson, and stood out from the rest of her face. She blinked, amazed by the sight.

'It's a start,' Angela said. 'We got to go, bus will be honking at us soon.'

Cassie hesitated, letting Angela leave the bathroom first. When she was alone, she took a tissue and wiped off some of the lipstick, so the effect was softer and not so startling. Then she hurried after her roommate, found her school-books, went downstairs to gulp down a few bites of breakfast, then joined the rest of the high school group in the front hall.

But she glanced covertly at Angela's oversize purse. Yes, it bulged and hung low from her arm, as if it were stuffed full. Angela was up to something.

But Cassie couldn't say anything, with the other girls all around and a counselor nearby. Not until the yellow school bus pulled into the drive and they had all climbed into the bus did she have a chance to speak.

Cassie sat down beside Angela. 'What are you going to do?' she whispered.

Angela's brown eyes narrowed. 'What you mean, girl?'

'I saw you putting extra clothes into your purse this morning; I heard you crying last night.'

Angela's lips tightened; she lifted her fist. 'If you rat on me –'

'I won't, I promise,' Cassie said quickly. 'What are you doing, Angela?'

'I got to see my baby.' Despite the roughness of her tone, Angela's eyes shone with tears again, and she blinked hard. 'She's still sick, she cries for me, and I don't want to be here, I want to be with my baby. I'm going home, that's all.'

'Where's home?' Cassie asked, keeping her voice low, too.

'Not too far; I can get there with no trouble,' Angela murmured. 'You just never mind; you keep your mouth shut, you hear?'

But this time, Cassie shook her head. 'No,' she told her roommate firmly. 'I want to go with you.'

'What?' Angela's eyes widened in surprise. 'What you want to go home with me for?'

'Not home with you, just away from the school; I have to find Seth. I think he's the one who hijacked the taxi,' Cassie whispered.

Angela looked at her with apparent respect. 'He's some bad dude.'

'No, he's not.' Cassie's voice had risen. She glanced around, but no one seemed to be listening to their conversation. The girl in the next seat dabbed her nose with a sponge from a small compact, and the two boys behind them were laughing loudly at some joke of their own.

She lowered her voice again. 'Seth is not a

criminal. But he's trying to find me, and I told him – well, something I said upset him. I need to find him before he gets into so much trouble he'll never get out.'

Angela sputtered, her lips curved in laughter. 'You talk about trouble; you thought about yourself, girl? This ain't no play school you're at. Think they'll just let you walk away? The court sent you here, right?'

Cassie nodded, a ripple of unease clouding her impulsive decision. 'If I run away, what will they do to me?'

Angela shrugged. 'Maybe just a slap on the wrist. But maybe not. They decide to call it 'escape,' then you went and committed a felony. That's big-time trouble, girl. You get sent to a heavy-duty lockup then.'

Was Angela exaggerating? Cassie wished she knew what was true and what was not. But Angela's eyes were grim, even when her lips curved into a bitter smile. 'So why are you doing it, then?'

'Told you, didn't I? My baby needs me, and they're not going to catch me again, not if I can help it,' Angela said, very low.

Cassie took a deep breath. 'They'll have to catch me, too, and maybe I can get to Seth first. He needs me, and he's in bigger trouble than I am; he stole a taxi and kidnapped the driver.'

Angela rolled her eyes. 'That's big, all right.

But nobody said you could go with me. You don't know nothing – you just slow me down, that's what.'

'If you don't let me go, I'll tell them what you're planning,' Cassie said calmly.

Angela glared at her, but Cassie met her eyes, refusing to look down. At last Angela shrugged. 'You'll be sorry, white girl.'

Cassie ignored the warning. Seth, she thought, I'm coming. Don't do anything else stupid. I'll find you, somehow.

The bus pulled up to the side of the school and the kids on board pushed and chattered as they filed out of the bus and up toward the front doors. Cassie followed Angela closely, keeping an eye on her movements.

As they entered the building, Cassie wondered how she would know when Angela made her move; they weren't in the same classes. What if Angela slipped away without her?

Then Cassie remembered; this morning regular classes had been canceled. There was a big assembly in the gym, some special program. Was that why Angela had chosen today to leave – because it would be harder to notice her absence, take longer to determine she wasn't in the school building?

Angela looked over her shoulder. 'You planning on being my shadow, huh?'

Cassie nodded, trying to look determined.

'You got it.'

'Then, come on, white girl, we see how smart you really are,' Angela muttered beneath her breath. She waited impatiently while Cassie put her schoolbooks into her locker, then the two made their way down the crowded hall. All the other students were making their way toward the gym, talking loudly, spirits high at this change in schedule.

'Here, got to make a stop,' Angela said. Cassie followed her into the girls' rest room, where two girls combed their hair in front of the mirrors, giggling over some private joke. Was this just a ploy?

But Angela went into a stall and pulled the door shut. Cassie leaned against a washbasin, prepared to wait. Maybe Angela was nervous, too. Cassie's own stomach felt as if it were tied in knots. Despite her final act of rebellion against her father, she was not accustomed to flouting authority. But Seth was in trouble.

The other two girls finished arranging their hair and went out, still talking. The rest room was silent.

Cassie suddenly noticed that she couldn't see Angela's feet beneath the bottom of the door. 'What are you doing?'

'Shush,' Angela said. 'They gone? You alone?'

'Yes,' Cassie said, mystified.

'Then go in a stall, dummy, lock the door, and

stand up on the toilet so no one can see you're inside.'

Cassie followed instructions, pushing the sliding lock on the door, then climbing awkwardly to stand on the chipped enamel seat. She felt very silly. 'Now what?'

'Button your lip,' Angela whispered fiercely. 'Now we wait, case someone checks.'

Sure enough, just as Cassie had decided this was an unnecessary precaution, she heard the outer door open and footsteps as someone entered the rest room.

She ducked her head farther down, hoping her heart wasn't pounding as loudly as she thought; she wondered if it might be heard outside the stall.

But it wasn't a teacher; she distinctly heard a muffled giggle, then a youthful voice saying, 'I'll watch the door; you light up first.'

She heard the sharp sound of a match, then smelled strong tobacco odors. But hardly had the first smoker begun her illicit cigarette than the other girl hissed, 'Someone's coming.'

Cassie heard the first girl's gasp, then a toilet flushing as the evidence disappeared.

'Come along, girls,' an older voice said. 'The program's about to start; you don't want to be late.'

'No, ma'am,' the second girl said meekly, and footsteps receded out the door.

Cassie had been holding her breath. After several long minutes, while the silence was unbroken, she heard a squeak as a stall door opened.

Angela whispered, 'No one here.' Cassie stepped down. Her arms were tired from bracing herself against the walls of the stall for so long; she felt like a criminal already.

'Thought those dummies were going to mess up my whole plan,' Angela grumbled. 'The teacher might have checked the stalls, then we'd be in a fine mess.

'Now what?' Cassie asked. 'Back out the side door?'

'Naw,' Angela said, glancing at her makeup in the mirror and touching her hair. 'Someone might see us. There's always a teacher in the hall. We're going out the window.'

Cassie turned and looked at the tall, narrow window high up against the outside wall. 'That? We can't.'

Angela grinned. 'Sure we can. You want to go with me, you can do your part, girl. Get the wastebasket.'

They pushed the heavy trash can under the window, then Angela climbed up, balancing herself on its flat top. She reached down to Cassie. 'Come on.'

'There's not enough room,' Cassie objected. But Angela was already pulling on her arm, and

Cassie managed to squeeze herself beside the other girl. 'We still can't reach the window.'

'You make a step with your hands, and I will,' Angela told her. She showed Cassie how to lace her fingers together and support the weight as Angela stepped up into her hands.

Cassie braced herself while the shorter girl reached to touch the window ledge. The glass windowpane slanted outward; it would be a tight squeeze to get through the opening. But Angela had swung herself over the ledge, balanced for a minute, then reached back for Cassie.

Cassie realized she'd been holding her breath, afraid Angela would leave her here. She took the hand Angela held out. She was taller than Angela and could just reach the window ledge. With Angela's help, she pulled herself up, feeling the strain in her arms and shoulders, but too desperate to give up now. Finally, she hung over the edge.

'I'm going out, then you follow,' Angela whispered. 'No room for both of us on this ledge.' Angela turned and slipped her legs through the narrow opening. Then she pushed herself through.

Cassie waited, eyes wide, hoping Angela made the drop to the outside without injury. This was crazy; they could break a leg, get into trouble with the school, with the girls' home.

Cassie might not even fit through the window opening. What if she got stuck, or what if the baby inside her was hurt by the fall?

But Seth was waiting, somewhere, risking his freedom, maybe his life, to find her.

Cassie took a deep breath, then pulled herself fully onto the window ledge. She turned, as Angela had done, and put her long legs through the opening.

'Oh, help,' she murmured, then slid farther. The window frame pressed painfully against her wider abdomen – was she stuck?

Cassie gulped hard; there was no going back. She had to get through it. She pushed harder, ignoring the pain from skin scraped raw by the metal frame. At last, she felt herself slip forward.

Gasping, she fell the rest of the way through the window, landing in a heap on the ground outside. She had gone down on top of a bush. The prickly leaves scratched her arms, but it probably helped break her fall, she thought.

Angela was already pulling her up. 'You okay? We got to make tracks. Come on.'

Feeling battered and bruised, Cassie followed the other girl in a fast trot toward the street.

Now, like Seth, she was a fugitive.

Chapter 12

Dear Diary,
I keep losing diaries. Now all I have is a little
notebook I was using to write homework assign-
ments in; it was in my jacket pocket. But when
I'm worried, I need to write something down.
I'm scared. What will happen if they catch us?
And what will happen if they don't, with no
family, and now not even the counselors at the
school to turn to? I'm on my own, and I've never
had to deal with people by myself. I always had
my father making the decisions. There are so
many things I don't know. If it weren't for
Angela –

'Come on,' Angela said impatiently. 'I said
you could rest a minute on the bench, but you
got to keep up. We got a long way to go. What
you writing down, anyhow?'

'Nothing,' Cassie said, flushing in embarrassment. She pushed the small notebook and the
pen back into her jacket pocket and stood up

again, stifling a sigh. They had been walking since they left the school over an hour ago. Her feet and legs and back were already tired.

But she stood up and followed Angela down the street again. They were walking past a row of small shops when Angela grabbed her arm. 'Cops!'

Cassie glanced back and saw the police car a block away. Her heart pounded; she felt cold all over. 'Are they looking for us?'

'Don't know, don't want to find out,' Angela muttered. 'In here.' She ducked into the closest shop door, and Cassie followed.

Inside, she smelled the starchy aroma of new clothes; elegant suits and beaded dresses hung from the racks. Looking around in bewilderment, Cassie saw that Angela was studying the dresses. She pretended to browse, too.

A saleslady dressed in prim navy blue came forward. She wore pearls in her ears, and her expression was suspicious, though her tone was polite. 'May I help you ladies find something?'

'We just looking,' Angela murmured.

But the saleslady hovered nearby, watching them.

Angela inspected a crimson evening dress and whispered to Cassie, 'Old cow, she thinks we shoplifting.'

'You mean stealing? Why would she?' Cassie felt indignant. But she examined one of the price tags – she didn't have the nerve to touch the dress itself, pale blue and spangled with sequins – and gasped. 'I didn't know dresses could cost so much,' she whispered back. 'No wonder; she knows we don't have the money to buy these.'

'Why not? Rich people wear jeans, too,' Angela murmured, her eyes bright with anger. 'Just because – oh.'

Cassie turned to the big front window and saw it, too. The police car cruised slowly past the shop.

Angela wandered toward the door. 'These dresses too old for me,' she said loudly. 'They got no style.'

Embarrassed, Cassie couldn't look at the saleslady. She ducked her head and followed Angela out of the shop. Taking a deep breath when they were on the sidewalk again, she glared at her roommate.

'What?' Angela looked innocent. 'Come on.' Twice more they had to duck into a doorway to avoid the gaze of a police officer. Angela seemed to be amazingly aware of the street and its occupants. The next store they entered was a small market, and Cassie looked longingly at the bins of fresh fruit; it was nearing lunchtime and her stomach felt very empty. No one had told her how hungry you could get when you were pregnant.

But they didn't linger long in that store, either. The man behind the counter looked them over. 'What are you doing out of school at this time of day?'

'I'm eighteen,' Angela said with pretended indignation. 'Don't have to go to school, nosy.' She grabbed Cassie's arm – Cassie couldn't think of any response – and they left the store quickly.

Cassie sighed. Running away was hard work. They kept walking.

After another hour, the nicer shops had been left behind and the neighborhood gradually became a little more littered, the storefronts less fancy, the windows streaked with dust.

Now there were other problems. As they walked past a concrete store wall covered with graffiti, Angela said sharply, 'Zip up your jacket, girl.'

Cassie looked at her in surprise. 'But I'm hot. With all this walking –'

'Unless you want to dump the sweater, you do what I say,' Angela retorted.

'What's wrong with my sweater?' Confused, Cassie looked down at the red sweater; it was one of the nicer ones she'd received from the clothing closet.

'Wrong color, that's what. You don't want to give some low-down gang boy an excuse to jump us.' Angela's tone was serious.

Looking around uneasily, Cassie zipped the

jacket up to her chin. 'How do you know all that, which gang is which neighborhood, I mean?'

'Saw the Signs,' Angela told her, nodding toward the graffiti. 'Communication is power, as the teacher say.'

Cassie grinned unwillingly and trudged on. 'Are we going to walk all the way, Angela? Where is your home? Is it in Knoxville?'

'Ask a lot of questions, don't you?' was Angela's only answer.

They walked several more blocks, then Angela led the way inside a small cafe'. Cassie sniffed the air, wishing intently for double servings of the whole menu. She felt totally hollow inside.

Angela pushed her toward a chair. 'Wait for me.'

Cassie sat down obediently, glad to rest. Her mouth was dry from the long walk, and her stomach felt as if it had a hole burrowed right through it.

A basket of crackers sat on the table. No one had approached her table; could she eat a cracker without anyone yelling? Her hunger made her queasy.

Cassie was too ravenous to resist. Darting her hand across the red and white oilcloth, she plucked a cellophane-wrapped cracker from the basket, pulled the plastic off, and stuffed the crackers in her mouth.

It didn't help her thirst, but even the little bit of food tasted good, and the saltiness steadied her stomach. Cassie ate another pack of crackers, and another, hoping no one would criticize.

She finally had the nerve to glance around the small diner. Angela stood at the counter, talking to a young black man who seemed pleased with her company; the two were laughing and chattering as if they were old friends. Maybe they were; there was still a lot she didn't know about Angela. Cassie looked at the other diners at the small tables and suddenly felt very self-conscious. She was the only white person in the place. She felt awkward and embarrassed at herself for not being at ease. Cassie stared at the tablecloth. Though her stomach still growled, she didn't reach for any more crackers. Maybe they wouldn't want her here.

Angela was coming back now with the young man beside her. He was taller than Angela, darkskinned, with an easy grin and bright brown eyes.

'Got us a ride, girl, the man's going our way. Come on, then,' Angela told her briskly.

Cassie was afraid to ask questions; she followed them outside the restaurant, leaving the savory smells behind with regret, and climbed into the pickup truck after Angela.

'This is Ed,' Angela said. 'This my friend from school,' she told him.

Cassie nodded; she was too shy to speak as he started the engine and they pulled into the street. At least they weren't walking anymore. She leaned back against the worn upholstery, glad to be sitting down, and tried to find a place for her feet among the cardboard boxes stacked on the floorboard.

Where were they headed? Out of town, apparently; they turned back toward the highway. Cassie watched the buildings flow by; before long they were surrounded by fields again and trees.

Where was Seth? The state was so big, how would she ever find him?

Angela and Ed chatted. Cassie admired her roommate's ease with this young man; she herself would have been tongue-tied with nervousness. When Ed lifted his right hand from the wheel and laid it on Angela's knee, Cassie tensed, alarmed for her friend.

Angela pushed his hand away. 'Don't get no ideas,' she told him, her tone matter-of-fact.

Ed frowned.

Cassie was torn between admiration for Angela's courage in standing up for herself and fear that he would put them down on the side of the highway.

But he soon smiled again. 'Can't blame a man for trying,' he told Angela. 'Not with a pretty girl like you.'

Angela grinned back at him, and their flirtatious banter continued.

Cassie sighed, watching the road signs. Where were they going?

When they reached the outskirts of the town of Oak Ridge, Ed turned off the highway and drove them through streets of small homes. Then he turned into a street filled with two-story apartments and stopped the truck.

'Thanks, brother,' Angela told him.

'You got some free time, give me a call,' he said hopefully. 'I'm in the book.'

At Angela's nod, Cassie opened the door and climbed awkwardly down from the high step.

'See you.' Angela waved, and Ed pulled away. Cassie followed Angela up the sidewalk. 'Are we there?'

Angela nodded, opening a screen door. They climbed one flight of stairs, and Angela knocked on the door.

Cassie could hear loud music playing inside the apartment. She waited, her heart fluttering nervously. What would Angela's family say about her running away from school? She tried to imagine her own family's response, thought of her father's rages, his loud voice and heavy hand. And what would they say about Angela bringing home a stranger? She wished she had somewhere else to go, but she didn't know where it would be. Her impulsive plan to find

Seth had seemed simple enough, when she first thought of it. Now – The door opened. A stout woman with dark skin and beautiful dark eyes stared at them in surprise. 'Angie, baby! What you doing here?'

'I'm home, Momma,' Angela said, hugging her mother with enthusiasm. 'How's Terri Lynn? She still sick? Did you get her to the doctor?'

'She's better. Mary down the street, she took us yesterday; we got her some antibiotics,' Angela's mother told her. 'The baby's taking a nap.

How come you out of that school? And who's this?'

Cassie flushed, not knowing what to say.

'This is my roommate, Momma, Cassie.'

'Lord, child, did you two run away from the school? What the judge going to say now?' Angela's mother seemed to have forgotten Cassie for the moment.

Instead of answering, Angela waved Cassie toward the purple flowered couch. 'Momma, we starving. What you got to eat?'

She pulled her mother toward the kitchen. Cassie sat down on the worn couch, but even with the loud music from the radio on the table, she could hear their voices.

'What you trying to do, get yourself in more trouble?' Mrs. Johnson's voice was hard-edged with anxiety. 'And bringing home this girl – you know how much food we got in the house! What you thinking of, child?'

Cassie heard Angela answer, 'She got no place to go, Momma,' then the voices lowered suddenly, and Cassie couldn't make out the words.

Cassie blushed with embarrassment. She knew it; she shouldn't have come. She shouldn't have started this whole crazy flight, except she was so worried about Seth. But she couldn't go back now, even if she had a way. What would she do?

When Angela and her mother came back out of the kitchen, Cassie jumped up. 'I'll be going now,' she said quickly, trying to keep her voice from trembling. 'I'm sorry; I shouldn't have come without asking.' She could feel tears behind her eyelids and a deep fear inside her; when she walked out that door, she had no notion where to go.

But Mrs. Johnson looked at her hard for a moment, then shook her head and opened her arms, just as she had hugged Angela earlier. 'Lordy, child, don't talk foolish.'

Cassie felt the woman's strong arms around her and tears overflowed. She laid her head on the broad chest for an instant, struggling for control.

'Now, don't take on.' Mrs. Johnson patted her

shoulder. 'I don't throw my children out, not like your folks. Angela got herself in trouble her own self, with her smart mouth and missing too much school.'

'Momma!' Angela protested.

'You two wash up and I'll get you something to eat,' Angela's mother said. 'I got some good stew and corn bread.'

'Thank you,' Cassie said. 'It sounds wonderful.'

'Just a minute,' Angela told them. 'I got to see my baby first. Come on, Cassie, I'll show you my angel.'

Cassie's stomach growled in protest, but she was curious. She followed Angela to the small bedroom where the little girl lay in her crib.

They tiptoed in and bent over the side. The little girl had chocolate-colored skin and wispy dark hair.

'What a little doll,' Cassie whispered. 'She's beautiful, Angela.'

Angela looked smug. 'I know. Terri Lynn, Momma's home. Wake up, baby.'

The little girl opened her eyes, blinked in confusion, then focused on Angela's face. 'Mommy!'

Angela pulled her up, hugged her tight. 'Oh, baby, I missed you *so* much.'

Cassie felt she was intruding; she backed up a little, but watched with eyes damp all over again and touched her own abdomen instinctively.

Angela talked and hugged and cooed and hugged, and the child laughed out loud. Finally Angela motioned toward Cassie. 'This is my friend. Say, 'Hi, Cassie.'"

'Hi, Cassie,' Terri Lynn repeated, grinning.

Cassie came closer to touch her cheek gently. 'Hi, Terri Lynn. You're awful pretty.' She smelled sweet, like baby powder, and her skin was soft and smooth. She wore a pink-flowered coverall, and had tiny rhinestone earrings in each ear.

'She my princess,' Angela said proudly. 'Aren't you, baby? Come on, let's go eat. I'm starved.'

Cassie didn't argue; she'd never felt so empty. In the small kitchen they crowded around the table and ate the stew and corn bread that Angela's mom offered. Cassie didn't want to eat too much, but it was hard – everything tasted so good.

When they finished, Cassie insisted on washing the dishes, despite the fatigue that made her arms heavy and slowed her steps. She had to do something in return for their hospitality.

Angela's mom looked at her thoughtfully and didn't argue. Angela took her little girl into the living room; she couldn't seem to get enough of her, and didn't want to put her down even for a moment. Her mother sat on the couch beside them, watching them both.

Cassie glanced through the doorway at them, then turned back to the sink. While she washed the dishes, she blinked back tears; so much love in that room. It made her feel even more lonely.

Despite the water running and the television blaring, Cassie could hear snatches of their conversation.

'You going to have to go back, Angela,' her mother said. 'You just get yourself in more trouble. What the judge say now?'

'Don't care,' Angela said stubbornly. 'I got to be with my baby. She going to grow up and forget who her momma is.'

'What about your schooling? You too smart to waste yourself, girl.'

'Don't care about school, neither,' Angela argued. 'My baby –'

'Don't do your baby no good if you can't get a decent job; you want to end up like me? Stuck in the projects working for minimum wage 'cause I dropped out of school?'

'I think you're smart, Momma,' Angela insisted.

Her mother made a harsh sound. 'Smart don't pay no rent. If you smart, you stay in school, and stay out of trouble with that judge.'

'No,' Angela repeated.

Cassie sighed and tried not to hear. When the

last dish was stacked, Cassie hung up the dish-cloth and joined them in the tiny living room. Mrs. Johnson looked at her.

'You look dead on your feet, child. You okay?'

'Just tired,' Cassie said.

'Yeah, me, too,' Angela agreed. 'We did a lot of walking today. Come on, let's go to bed.'

'I want to see the news first, please,' Cassie told them, looking at the clock on the wall.

Mrs. Johnson looked puzzled, but Angela nodded and turned the channel.

They didn't have long to wait. 'The kid-napped taxi driver has been found; he escaped his captor and flagged down a truck on Interstate 40. The taxi and the young man who hijacked it are still missing. Coming up, the weather.'

Cassie blinked, disappointment heavy inside her.

Angela put one arm around her shoulders.

'Get some sleep, girl,' she said gently. 'We listen again in the morning; more news then, maybe.'

Cassie nodded, wanting to cry. Oh, Seth, she thought. Where are you?

Chapter 13

Dear Cassie,

I've had another delay, but I'm still on my way. I meant what I said about being there for you and the baby. I couldn't stand for him to feel the way I did when I was a kid. It's pretty bad knowing your old man didn't care enough to hang around, that maybe you even drove him away.

I want my baby, Cassie, and I want you. I don't know when you'll get this – I hope to see you in a few hours. But if I don't, because they'll have to kill me to stop me, Cassie, maybe someone will send you this letter.

At least you'll know how much I loved you, and that I tried.

Seth

He drove for a few miles, then came to a crossing where an even smaller road crossed the twolane blacktop. Seth braked, wondering which way to go. He hadn't seen any other traffic, and the loneliness of the landscape was almost unnerving for someone brought up within the comforting protection of city limits, even those of a small town.

Seth let the motor idle while he pulled the map from his pocket and tried to figure out where he was. But the road was too small and the scope of the map too large; he couldn't identify his location.

Muttering a few words Cassie would not have approved of, Seth tossed the map onto the floor of the cab. He would have to make a guess. This road seemed to be heading north, and the smaller road snaked its way east, he thought.

Seth examined the gas gauge one more time. He should have enough gas to get to Knoxville, if he didn't waste it going the wrong direction and have to backtrack too many times. Seth pounded the wheel with his hands, but that only made his palms smart. Which way?

He was getting sleepy again, as the emotional charge of the confrontation with the taxi driver wore off. Seth rubbed his eyes and made a decision. He turned the cab into the smaller road and headed east.

The road wandered up and down increasingly steep hills, and Seth had to pay close attention to the small road; it turned and dipped unexpectedly, and there were few markings. And his eyelids were drooping; he found it harder and harder to focus on the narrow road.

He made it another mile, then his chin dropped suddenly. Seth fought to stay awake and had to jerk the wheel to avoid hitting a tree. The near miss sent adrenaline jolting through him and woke him up again, momentarily, but Seth knew his brief alertness wouldn't last. He had to find a place to pull off the road and nap a little, or he'd crash the cab back here in the boonies where no one would find him, and Cassie would never know how he'd tried to reach her, help her.

Then he looked back at the dash, and he blinked in dismay. The temperature gauge had jumped steeply, nearing the red zone. Now what?

Seth stopped in the middle of the road, got out, and lifted the hood. Steam sizzled past the radiator cap, and he knew enough not to try to open it now; he'd get scalded. Was the water in the radiator low? Maybe a city cab wasn't up to climbing steep mountain roads all day.

He needed to let the engine cool, and he needed some rest, anyhow. But where? He restarted the cab, watching the road and the temperature arrow as the vehicle crawled along. Seth couldn't find any place wide enough to pull off, the trees crowded the narrow road and left no clearance. Finally he saw a wider spot at the side of the road where only tall weeds grew.

With a sigh of relief, he pulled the cab onto the grass and turned off the engine. He lay back against the worn seat; just being able to shut his eyes without fear of a crash was a great luxury. Seth's mind drifted, and he slept.

He woke with a start – someone was chasing him. It was his mom's new boyfriend, flicking his cigarette lighter. Then Cassie had been calling for him, from somewhere just out of sight, with a baby's cries drowning out her voice – Seth had to swallow hard to hold back his fear.

For a moment the dream was so vivid that he didn't know where he was. Confused, he looked around at the tall trees that blocked any view of the horizon. The sun had dropped behind the hill, and shadows made the cab's interior gloomy.

A sudden far-off wail sent shivers down his spine. He thought wildly of a baby lost in the woods, then realized that it was no human voice he heard, though it must have invaded his dreams. That was an animal's cry, and it made him shiver.

Seth turned to check that the door was locked and the window rolled up. It was only a dog, Seth told himself, trying to be calm. But the distant howl was joined by another, and another, and the chorus sounded wild, feral, dangerous.

All of Seth's memories had flooded back, and he thought uneasily of the taxi driver, tied helplessly to a tree. What if the dogs attacked the bound man, and the driver couldn't defend himself – Seth felt sick at even considering such a possibility.

No way, he told himself. He'd slept longer than he meant to, exhausted by a night with little sleep and an eventful morning. The driver had probably pulled himself free by now, walked back to the interstate, and flagged down a ride.

But if not – it would be Seth's fault. Seth fought with the impulse to go back and check on the man. But it would waste more time, and might lead him into the clutches of the police. Besides, Cassie needed him more.

Seth squared his shoulders. If the driver was loose, the police might already be looking for him. He had to get going. He checked the temperature gauge; the arrow had dropped, but he wondered how long before it overheated again. Seth listened hard, but the dogs' howls had stopped. He got out of the cab, lifted the hood, and unscrewed the radiator cap.

It was hard to be sure, but he thought the water level was low. He inspected the hoses, finally spotting a drip at the bottom. The hose was leaking. Great.

Seth went to the trunk and rummaged

through it, finding some black electrical tape. He taped the hose, hoping this would stop the leak. But he still needed water to fill the radiator, or it would overheat all over again, and the engine could stop completely. Where could he find water? Seth slammed the hood down and got back behind the wheel.

Seth started the engine, turned the cab back onto the narrow road, and resumed his slow progress. He couldn't go too fast; he didn't want to press the engine too hard, and besides, there were too many unexpected curves and dips. The sunlight was fading fast.

He had probably taken the wrong road, Seth told himself, cursing his ineptitude. Should he turn around and go back to the crossroads? But how would he know which way to go next? And he needed water. Seth slowed the vehicle even further, glancing anxiously at the temperature gauge, when he saw the weed-choked driveway and the house set back up against the trees.

Did someone live here? Could he ask directions, or would the residents have heard from TV reports that he was a fugitive and report him?

Seth pulled into the driveway, but didn't approach the house any closer. What should he do?

As he debated, he saw the front door open,

and an elderly lady look out. She didn't appear dangerous. She had wispy gray hair pulled up at the back of her head, and a faded cotton dress, with an apron over it where she dried her hands as she peered uncertainly toward the drive.

Seth inched the cab closer, then turned off the motor and stepped out.

'Excuse me, could you tell me the right road to get to Knoxville?'

He wasn't sure she had heard. Seth walked closer, looking around cautiously. He hadn't heard any dogs bark, but you never knew.

'Could you tell me the road to Knoxville?' he repeated.

She didn't seem to see him until he stood at the bottom of the steps.

'Oh, I thought maybe you was the repairman,' she said, disappointment in her tone. 'Lost, are you?'

'Yes, ma'am. If you could just tell me the road and let me have a little water for my engine? It's overheating.'

'Water, well, that's a problem right now,' she told him. 'I'll see what I have.'

Now that he was up close, Seth saw that her eyes were cloudy, strange-looking, and she peered hard at him when he spoke. But she had a mild voice, overlaid with a twangy mountain accent, and her wrinkled face looked good-natured.

She opened the screen door. 'Wipe your feet,' she told him as if he were a child. 'And come on in.'

He wiped his sneakers on the worn mat and followed her inside. The small house was painfully neat, though the couch had bare patches on the ancient velvet cushions and he saw a crack in the wallpaper behind the chair. A gray cat sleeping on the chair opened its green eyes and jumped to its feet, its hair rising in alarm at the sight of a stranger. The animal streaked away to hide beneath the sofa. Seth saw no television, not even a radio.

The old woman kept going, through the front room to the kitchen behind it. This room also gleamed with cleanliness, though the electric stove and refrigerator were years past their prime, and some of the blue and white dishes stacked on the open shelves were chipped. A big pot bubbled on the stove, and the savory aroma that filled the room made Seth pause on the threshold. His empty stomach growled audibly at the wonderful smells, and he flushed in embarrassment.

'Hungry? Sit yourself down and have a bite to eat,' she told him.

'I couldn't eat your dinner, but thank you for the offer,' Seth told her. His refusal didn't sound convincing, even to him; he'd almost forgotten the last time his stomach had been really full. He'd been hungry for so long it had begun to seem a normal condition.

'Shoot, I got plenty. You're just a boy, and boys are always hungry. I raised four; I should know. You pull up a chair.' She motioned toward the wooden table and took a plate from the cupboard.

Seth didn't argue anymore; his mouth was already watering. He watched her spoon stewed chicken and a mass of dumplings from the pot on the stove, filling the plate to capacity before she set it in front of him. She found a fork for him, then poured him a glass of milk from the fridge.

'Eat up,' she said. 'What's your name? I'm Martha Ann Wilson.'

Seth hadn't waited for the urging. 'S-Sam,' he mumbled, his mouth full, remembering that he was a fugitive. The flat, tender dumplings tasted incredibly good, and the savory chicken as well. He'd never had a better meal in his life, Seth thought, stuffing it in. He didn't try to talk anymore, simply enjoyed the food, eating rapidly until he had scraped the plate clean. He drank the last of the milk and took a deep breath.

'Thank you, ma'am. That was awfully good. Could I get some water, now?'

She smiled at his praise. 'I'll have to get more water, Sam. I used the last in the bucket.'

He saw that although a white sink stood

against the wall, she was peering into a pail of water on the counter.

'My pump quit,' she explained. 'Been having to draw water from the old spring up the hill, least till I can get a repairman out this far. He was supposed to come yesterday, but he didn't show up.'

Seth looked at the empty pail and her thin, fragile-looking frame. 'You've been carrying water in a bucket?'

'Over a week,' she told him, sighing. 'Don't know what's wrong with the dratted pump this time. Can't see it that well, to tell the truth. It's these cataracts.'

Seth tried not to stare at her eyes; that explained their milky appearance. 'That's bad. Can't they do something to help?'

'Oh, the doctor in town's been fussing about surgery, but I ain't made up my mind to that, not yet,' she told him. She picked up the empty pail.

Seth jumped to his feet. 'Here, ma'am. I'll do that.'

He took the aluminum bucket and followed her out the back door and through a screened-in porch. She picked up a walking stick on the back porch. Inside, Seth realized, she had the small house memorized, but outside, walking was more difficult because of her limited vision.

Using the stick to feel her way, she led him up

a small path. There were branches and twigs scattered here and there, and small trees were uprooted. Seth looked at the debris in surprise.

'What happened?'

'Had a little twister during that storm last week,' she told him. 'Lucky it didn't hit the house, but it knocked the trees around.'

'You must have been scared,' he said, looking at her with new admiration. She looked too old and frail to live out here all alone.

'Hid in the root cellar,' she admitted, grinning at him, though she couldn't seem to focus on him clearly. 'Me and Columbus.'

'Columbus?'

'My cat. There's my well and the pump house.' She pointed to a bend in the path, and Seth stopped to look. A tree had fallen into the small structure, breaking through the frame shed that protected the machinery; no wonder the electric pump had stopped working.

'There's a tree down on it. Let me take a look.' Seth sat the bucket down, then braced himself to pull the heavy limbs away from the pump. In a few minutes he had the trunk out of the way. Puffing with the effort, he cleared out more branches and fragments of splintered wood, then put aside the fallen shingles from the roof of the pump house. He opened the small door and sank to his knees, trying to see what might have stopped the pump. Was it major damage, or only something that had jammed the machinery?

'Do you have a large screwdriver, ma'am, and a flashlight?' It was really dark now, and he couldn't see enough to assess the damage.

'Sure do,' she said promptly. 'You wait here; I'll be right back.'

He peered into the pump until she returned, tapping her walking stick briskly, unfazed by the darkness. She handed Seth the flashlight and two screwdrivers, and he turned the light onto the pump, then lay on his stomach in the dirt while he adjusted the motor.

He worked for half an hour, then flicked a switch, and the motor suddenly hummed with life. 'I think it's working again,' Seth said, pleased that he'd done something right. 'Now I need to get some water in my radiator and get going.'

'I sure do appreciate your help, Sam. You know, it's mighty dark on these mountain roads, especially with you being lost. I've got a cot on the back porch; I sleep there sometimes in the summer when it's hot. You can have it for the night, if you want, then get an early start in the morning.'

Seth hesitated. He had already spent too much time here. But he was far away from the highway, out of sight from prying eyes, and the old lady couldn't even see the stolen cab.

'All right,' he decided. 'Thank you, I will.'

She gave him blankets, let him use her small bathroom – obviously delighted that the taps now produced water once more – and left him to curl up on the narrow cot. It was a better bed than he'd had the night before, Seth thought. Where was Cassie sleeping tonight; did she think he'd never come? And were the police still watching the interstate for him?

Could he elude them long enough to find Cassie? Maybe he should get rid of the taxi, which was so easy to spot – but then how would he make it to the girls' school in Knoxville? Too many problems.

Even with all the questions running through his mind, Seth drifted into sleep, turning restlessly once when he heard the distant howling.

He woke early, and found that Mrs. Wilson was already up and insisted on feeding him breakfast.

Seth ate the fluffy biscuits, country ham and gravy, and scrambled eggs eagerly. The old woman watched him with apparent pleasure, sipping a cup of black coffee, her plate already pushed back.

'I heard a dog howling last night,' he told her when he finished as he wiped his mouth on a gingham napkin. 'Sounded like more than one, in fact.'

She nodded. 'It's a pack of dogs, strays and

abandoned pets gone wild. Farmers round here been trying to track them down all winter. They killed some pigs two farms over.' She shook her head at the thought.

Seth shivered, then concentrated on more pressing matters. 'Thank you for the breakfast, ma'am. It was really good. Now can you tell me which road to take to get to Knoxville?'

'You sure did get yourself lost, didn't you? Easiest way is to go back to the interstate,' she told him. 'Nothing up this road but the radio tower and my boys' hunting cabin – they come up from the city in the fall, always spend Thanksgiving with me.' Her wrinkled face creased into a wide smile at the thought.

'Is there another way?' Seth asked, hoping she wouldn't think his question odd.

'If you don't want to backtrack that far, go back to the last crossroad, take a right on the county road, then at the foot of the hill, go right again. When you come to a gray church, take the left fork and it'll get you over the mountain, and you'll see signs back to the state road.'

Seth frowned in concentration. 'I sure thank you,' he told her. 'For everything.'

'I appreciate the help fixing my pump,' she said. 'You're a good boy, Sam. Your mother must be proud of you.'

Her wrinkled face was so innocently kind that Seth had to swallow hard. 'I-I hope so,' he murmured. 'Good-bye.'

He refilled the radiator of the cab with clean water, then retraced his route to the crossroads, and set out to follow the route she'd suggested.

He drove for some time without seeing another vehicle, but when he passed the church, a man in a pickup truck stared at him, and Seth felt very conspicuous in the bright yellow city cab out in the middle of the mountainside.

He drove on, hoping for the best, but when he rounded another rise in the road, Seth's heart seemed to leap into his mouth – he saw the distinct markings of a sheriff's car just ahead.

The sheriff was leaning against his patrol car; had he been on the watch for Seth? Or for the cab, more likely, if the police had been alerted – they'd had time enough if the driver had gotten free.

Seth pressed his foot down on the gas pedal, and the cab sped forward. But he saw the uniformed man jump into the patrol car. The sheriff was coming after him!

How could he get away? The sluggish cab motor would never be able to outrun a police car over mountain roads.

Seth rounded one curve, then another, and for a moment he was out of his pursuer's sight. Seth saw a small dirt road turn off the blacktop, and without stopping to consider – there was no time – he turned the wheel sharply and pulled into the small byway.

It wasn't the right way, but if he could just escape the sheriff's attention, it would be worth the risk of getting lost again.

He stopped the car and cut the engine, listening hard. Yes, Seth heard the sound of a car flying along the blacktop; it didn't slow down; his evasive action wasn't as yet suspected.

Seth waited till the other car was out of earshot, then restarted the cab's engine and drove as fast as he dared down the narrow road – it was hardly more than two muddy ruts cutting through the brush. But it might take him away from the pursuit, and if he could get back to the main road a different way – so much the better.

He drove even faster, while tree branches slapped at the cab and reached through the half open window, making him duck. Bouncing and jolting over the rough road, Seth fought to keep control of the cab. He had to get away while he could, Seth told himself; he had to stay out of sight Cassie was waiting.

He went over a rise and then the road dipped downward. Seth's eyes widened. His foot pushed hard against the brake pedal, but the cab was going too fast.

The rough track had ended abruptly; it fell

away straight into the steep banks of a small mountain stream.

Seth shouted, but the sound was lost in the crashing as the cab slid down the bank, splintering small trees in its path before hitting the water. Seth felt the splash through the half open window and was thrown heavily against the wheel.

Stunned from the impact, Seth fought to focus his eyes. Blackness whirled at the edge of his vision, and then everything went dark.

Chapter 14

Dear Diary,

I'm so tired and so discouraged. Angela said I could sleep in her bed; they don't have any extra. I feel terrible at imposing on her mom, but I don't know what to do. I wouldn't have made it this far without Angela, and I still don't know where Seth is. But I have this awful feeling that he's getting into more and more trouble; I feel as if we're both caught in a tornado that will whirl us away, no matter what we do, and worst of all, we're being torn in different directions. Oh, Seth, I miss you.

Cassie lay very still, afraid to move in case she disturbed Angela, who lay beside her on the double bed. But after Terri Lynn was tucked safely into her crib, Angela appeared to fall asleep quickly, too. Cassie could hear Angela's even breathing, and the light whistle of the still congested baby from the opposite wall of the bedroom.

Cassie thought she might be unable to sleep, with all the worries on her mind and her unfamiliar surroundings. But she was so exhausted that very soon her eyes closed.

She awakened to wailing in the darkness. Confused, Cassie tried to pull herself fully awake. She was still so exhausted that she felt groggy, as if she'd been hit on the head. Pregnancy seemed to make her sleep harder, and the day behind them had had so many physical and mental strains.

Who was crying? She tried to sort it out, but Angela was already climbing out of bed, running to the crib.

'What's the matter, baby?'

Cassie should help. With great effort, she pushed herself up, staggered toward the crib. 'What's wrong?'

Angela flipped the light switch, and Cassie blinked against the sudden light. She also wrinkled her nose.

'Oh, lordy,' Angela muttered. 'She been sick all over the place. Momma!'

Cassie put one hand over her nose; her stomach, still often queasy, threatened to rebel. When Mrs. Johnson appeared wrapped in a bright robe, she was glad to step back and let the older woman take her place beside the baby's bed. Terri Lynn was still crying, and Angela made soothing noises, patting the baby on the back.

'What's wrong, Momma? She sick again! Maybe that doctor at the clinic don't know enough,' Angela told her mother, worry sharpening her tone.

Cassie wrapped her arms uselessly around her stomach, while Mrs. Johnson shook her head.

'She probably got a stomach upset from the antibiotics; it happens. We have to call the clinic tomorrow. Right now, let's get her cleaned up. You take her into the bathroom; I'll change the sheets. Hope I got a clean set; didn't have money for the Laundromat this week.'

But her voice was calm, and some of the fear in Angela's face subsided. She wrapped the toddler in a blanket and carried her toward the bathroom.

With nothing to contribute, Cassie got out of the way and went into the living room. Sitting on the edge of the couch, she shivered in the cool night air, not bothering to turn on a light. She took a deep breath; at least the baby wasn't seriously ill. What would Angela have done without her mother to steady her, offer advice?

Cassie touched her own stomach, felt the quiver of the life growing inside her. What would Cassie do when the baby was born, and her own family was not there to offer help and support?

True, she'd helped care for her little sisters

and brother over the last few years, washing faces and making sandwiches and helping with schoolwork. But when they were born, she'd been too young to remember very much. She didn't know a lot about little babies.

If Cassie kept her baby, who would she turn to in the middle of the night when sudden illness struck? She'd have to face the fears, the uncertainties all alone. Her eyes filled with tears at the thought; she was afraid, already.

Trying to block out all the worries, she jumped up and went to look in the bathroom, where Angela had stripped her daughter and put her into the bathtub.

'Can I help?'

'Look in the bureau and see if you can find clean pajamas,' Angela said over her shoulder, holding firmly to the soapy baby. 'No, Terri Lynn, you can't eat the soap, honey.'

Cassie nodded and went to look. But she searched the drawers without luck, finally returning with a large T-shirt with a hole in the seam. 'I can't find anything else; will this do?'

'Have to, I guess.' Angela sighed and wiped a drop of water off her cheek. 'Here, Terri Lynn, don't cry again, baby.'

She dried the little girl, put on a clean diaper and the T-shirt, then took her back to bed.

'Can't find no more sheets,' Mrs. Johnson came back to tell them, sounding tired herself.

'It's okay; I want to keep her beside me, anyway,' Angela said. 'You mind, Cassie?'

'Of course not,' Cassie said. 'I'll go lie down on the couch.'

Angela gave her a blanket from the bed and Cassie took it back to the living room. Wrapping herself as well as she could against the chilly air, she lay down across the sofa.

Her makeshift bed wasn't very comfortable, but it could be worse. Where was Seth sleeping tonight? He might be on the ground somewhere, or maybe still in the taxicab. By comparison, the couch didn't seem so bad. She shut her eyes.

Someone was tugging on her hair. Half awake, Cassie tried to think if the puppy they'd once owned had returned; he was a sweet thing, but mischievous, and chewed on everything, nipping her toes when she lay in bed. But her father had gotten angry and taken him to the pound after a few weeks, she remembered with a pang.

She forced her eyes open. A little dark-eyed girl stared at her from only a few inches away.

'Hi,' the toddler said.

Where was she? Confused, Cassie blinked at the tiny face and the room around her, then memory rushed back. 'Hi, Terri Lynn,' she answered. 'You feel better?'

The child grinned. Cassie sat up on the couch. She folded her blanket and went to the bedroom to pull on her sweater and jeans and shoes. She'd slept in her T-shirt and underwear and socks. Where was Angela?

Cassie found her roommate in the bathroom on her knees beside the tub, scrubbing small clothes by hand in sudsy water.

'Hi, sleepyhead,' Angela told her. 'How you feel?'

'Okay. Terri Lynn looks better,' Cassie said. 'Where's your mom?'

Angela wiped her forehead with the back of her arm instead of her soapy hand. 'Gone to work. She gets paid today. She's going to give me some money, then I'm out of here. They'll know were missing from McNaughten by now; cops or a social worker'll probably show up here soon looking for me.'

Cassie felt a flicker of alarm. Angela always had a plan. What was Cassie going to do? She couldn't hang on to Angela's coattails forever, and this wasn't bringing her closer to Seth.

'Morning news is on,' Angela told her. 'You said you wanted to listen.'

Cassie ran back to the television and turned up the volume. At first there was no mention of the taxi and its hijacker, but after the first headlines, the announcer added, 'And the missing taxicab has been sighted north of Fork

Mountain. Police are setting up roadblocks and expect to apprehend the hijacker shortly. The taxi driver has furnished police with a description of the alleged assailant.'

The drawing on the screen had Seth's long face, arched brows, the familiar strand of blond hair that dipped onto his forehead. He looked angry and menacing in the sketch, not how she was accustomed to seeing him. But any lingering doubts that it was Seth who had taken the taxi disappeared. It was him – she recognized the face even though it was distorted by someone else's fear and resentment, and he was in big trouble. She had to find him, keep him from getting himself killed. Roadblocks meant police, police with guns.

She was trembling when Angela came into the room. Cassie hugged herself, barely able to speak. 'It's Seth, all right. They said north of Fork Mountain. I've got to get there. I'll have to try to hitch a ride.'

Angela shook her head. 'Girl, you'll be eaten alive if you try to hitch. Wait a minute, that's not too far from here. I think I know someone who might be going that way. First, you need to eat something.'

Cassie couldn't deny that her stomach was hollow again. They ate toast and dry cereal in the kitchen; dry because there was only enough milk left for the baby. It was a strange meal, but it tasted good to Cassie. She rushed through it, asking Angela through a mouth full of bread, 'Who do you know who goes to Fork Mountain?'

In answer, Angela went to the telephone and picked up the receiver but shook her head. 'Dead,' she said matter-of-factly. 'Momma didn't have money for the bill, I guess. Come on, we try next door.' She gave Cassie another piece of bread, and Cassie chewed on it absently as she followed. Angela picked up Terri Lynn – she still didn't seem to want to be parted from her – and positioned the toddler on one hip.

Cassie grabbed her jacket – she had nothing to take, except the clothes on her back and the notebook in her pocket – and hurried after her. Angela knocked on the next apartment door. When the lady answered, she asked to use her neighbor's phone, while Cassie hovered nearby, tense with anticipation.

'He hasn't left yet,' Angela said when she hung up. 'Come on, we'll meet him at the corner.'

With hurried thanks to the elderly lady who lived next door, the two girls went back outside, Terri Lynn still riding snugly on her mother's hip.

'Who is this person – another neighbor?' Cassie asked faintly. On what stranger was she risking her flight and freedom this time? But she could hardly afford to be particular.

'Frank's okay, owns his own vending company, snacks, you know, small-time, but he covers a lot of little towns around the area,' Angela said. 'He don't live in the projects no more, owns his own house now. My momma's known him since they was kids.' She sounded faintly envious of his good fortune, but admiring, too.

Cassie nodded, somewhat reassured. They walked down the sidewalk to the street and headed for the next corner.

'Where are you going, Angela? Will you be okay?' Cassie asked her friend, thinking of how much she owed her.

Angela nodded. 'I got an aunt in – Well, better not say, better if you don't know if someone asks, later. But she'll take me in, I think. I want to take Terri Lynn and lie low for a while, stay out of sight and maybe they get off my back. I just want to be with my baby; I'll worry about school, later.'

They stood on the corner, Angela watching the traffic that zipped by, Cassie with her head down against the spring breeze that tossed her hair. 'I don't know how to thank you, Angela. If I make it, if I find Seth in time, it will be because of you. You've been great.'

Angela brushed her words aside, looking

uncomfortable. 'Shoot, girl, you such a baby, someone have to keep you straight,' she said. Then she frowned.

'What's wrong?' Cassie looked, too, but saw no police car or other apparent danger. Instead, a white panel truck with FRANK'S SNACKS on the side pulled to the curb.

'Hi, Frank,' Angela said to the driver, a middle-aged black man with grizzled hair. 'This my friend Cassie. She need a ride up to Fork Mountain.'

He looked at them both. 'You not going to get me in any trouble, are you?'

'No, sir,' Cassie told him, hoping it was true. 'Just a ride, that's all I want.'

He motioned to the door, and Angela helped her pull it open.

Cassie gave her friend a brief hug. 'I hope I see you again,' she whispered. 'Thanks for everything.'

Then she stepped into the truck.

Chapter 15

Dear Diary,

What if I can't find Seth before the police do, what will they do to him? He could be shot – even killed! There's no one here to explain that he's not a criminal, he's not a bad person. He's just desperate; he only wants to find me. Why does it seem as if everyone's trying to keep us apart? All we wanted was a chance to love each other – was that so bad?

It was hard to write with the van bouncing. Cassie put her little notebook back into her jacket pocket. She felt shy and awkward; she didn't know what to say to the driver as they rolled along the highway.

She looked around the van. Everything was carefully placed; the back was full of boxes, stacked and labeled, and a clipboard beside the driver's seat held sheets of papers and a pen. Taped neatly to the dash were wallet-sized school photos of three children, all small and dark-skinned, all wearing broad grins.

Cassie examined the smiling faces and somehow felt better. 'Your children?' she asked the driver.

'Grandchildren,' he told her.

Cassie looked at him in surprise; he didn't seem old enough to have grandchildren in elementary school. Her thoughts must have been apparent on her face, because Frank chuckled.

'I started too young, just like Angela,' he explained. 'Kids that age got no sense – and I was just the same. But I didn't run out on my girl, not like Angela's boyfriend. We got married, I worked my tail off, and in time, we got ahead. I got a nice little business now, and I built it up myself, from scratch. But a lot of people don't make it, starting so young. They end up divorced, bitter, or, like Angela, alone from the start, raising that poor baby all by herself.'

'Angela's a good mother,' Cassie protested. 'She loves her little girl.'

'She don't have it easy, though. I told my kids, you go to school, don't fool around, don't get married till you got a good start on life,' he told her, his tone kind but paternal.

'Yes,' Cassie murmured. She couldn't help putting one protective hand over her abdomen. The big loose sweater and the jacket still cloaked her own pregnancy. But the knowledge that she hadn't waited, hadn't 'had sense,' made her cheeks flush.

She stared out the front window of the truck, hoping he wouldn't notice her embarrassment. 'Your grandchildren are nice-looking kids.'

Fortunately, this succeeded in diverting his thoughts. 'They's smart as crackers, too,' he told her. 'Doing good in school. Their dad, my oldest, he bought them a computer to use at home, they got that thing figured out already. Josie, that's the middle one, she says she going to teach her old grandpa how to do the billing on it.'

He chuckled, and Cassie grinned, glad for the change in subject.

'You know about computers?'

'No.' Cassie shook her head. 'I wish I did; my old school had computers in one class, but I only got to stay at the school a few weeks, so I didn't really learn much.'

'They're something,' Frank told her. 'And the games, wow. My grandson, he can whip those space invaders.'

He told her stories of his grandkids until he pulled into a small gas station and turned off the engine. Cassie waited while he checked his clipboard and went around to open the back door to pull out the necessary supplies. Then, his arms loaded, he went in to restock.

Cassie thought about Seth, wondered if she would be able to find him. Just where was he, north of Fork Mountain? Maybe she'd never track him down; maybe the police would find him first. She wondered if there was any more news.

When Frank returned and pulled the vehicle back on the road, she asked shyly, 'Do you mind if we turn on the radio?'

'Sure, a little music would be fine.' He switched on the radio, and a country western song blared from the speakers.

They listened to the tunes as they rode, Frank sometimes humming along. Frank stopped often at small gas stations and little shops. Cassie wondered just how long it would take to reach her destination. Finally, the songs and ads and silly deejay patter paused, and a news break came on. Cassie stared resolutely out the window, trying not to make it obvious how eagerly she listened.

She waited impatiently through talk of a local mayor's race and a fire that had destroyed a garage. Then the announcer said, 'Traffic may be slow as police set up roadblocks in several locations around the area. State police say they are confident they will soon apprehend the hijacker; the stolen cab has been sighted twice near Fork Mountain.'

'Just my luck,' Frank muttered. 'I'm going right through all the roadblocks – roads will be a mess.'

The announcer continued on to another topic, and Cassie found that her hands were clenched into tight fists. She forced herself to relax, not wanting Frank to suspect. But he didn't seem to be watching her, he was pulling the van into another small station and cafe.

'I'm going to get a bite of lunch; you want to come?' he asked.

'I'll wait, my grandmother will probably have a meal cooking.' Cassie had no money, and she hoped he wouldn't offer to pay. She couldn't keep depending on the charity of strangers.

He looked thoughtfully at her. 'Suit yourself. Oh, there's a box behind your seat – damaged merchandise. Help yourself if you want a snack. I can't sell them like that, you know.'

He unloaded several boxes from the back of the truck, then went whistling into the station. When he was out of sight, Cassie couldn't resist turning to look at the box he'd mentioned. She found it half full of an assortment of packaged snacks, all crushed or dented in some way.

Her stomach rumbled at the sight of the food, even if it was only crackers and cookies and little cakes. Cassie selected a pair of chocolate cupcakes, and two packages of crackers and peanut butter. They were all broken or smashed, and she had to pick up the pieces carefully, but the food tasted just as good, and it made a dent in her hunger. She was glad Frank wasn't there to see how ravenously she ate.

By the time he returned, she had put the trash carefully into the litter bag he kept behind the seat and brushed the crumbs off her sweater. When he climbed back into the truck, he handed her an unopened pint carton of milk.

'Thought you might need something to wash it down,' he told her matter-of-factly. 'Where's your grandma live?'

'Thanks,' Cassie murmured. 'Not too far, now, she's out in the country a ways.' The milk was cold and tasted good; she drank it slowly, relishing the coolness against her parched throat.

He didn't ask any more. Frank started the truck and they set out again. Cassie was getting impatient now, and she sighed at every stop. She got out a couple of times to use the ladies' room; that was another thing about being pregnant. But within an hour, Frank had to slow the van because traffic on the narrow two-lane highway had crawled to a stop.

Cassie saw police cars ahead. She tensed. These must be the roadblocks set up to look for Seth. Would they be on the lookout for her as well, if McNaughten had reported her absence? How much trouble was she in?

'Shoot, I'll be all night finishing my rounds at this rate,' Frank grumbled.

Cassie glanced at him quickly, then back to

the road, thankful he didn't seem to notice her own agitation. She took a deep breath and tried to stay calm. She could slip out of the van and try to get around the police cars without being seen. But Frank would surely be suspicious if she ran away, now. Would he tell on her? Would he worry about his own involvement with a possible fugitive?

She hated to repay all his kindness this way.

The line of trucks and cars crawled slowly forward. Then a car stalled; it was two vehicles in front of them. From her high seat in the van, Cassie could see the elderly man behind the wheel try without luck to restart his engine. Behind them, cars honked and one truck driver yelled out his window.

Frank shook his head. 'What a mess.' He shut off his own engine and opened the door.

Alarmed again, Cassie saw him walk forward to confer with the harried policeman who was trying to get the disabled car moving again, while drivers honked and fumed in an increasingly long line behind them.

Cassie slouched lower in her seat, watching Frank and the police officer talk. She couldn't hear what they were saying. Was Frank talking about her? Did he suspect she was a runaway? Would he turn her in?

The policeman glanced toward the van. Cassie could hardly breathe. She thought wildly of jumping out of the van, running across the fields, but that would only confirm their suspicions. She gripped the edge of the seat and tried not to give in to her panic.

But then the policeman nodded, and Frank walked back, climbing into the van.

'They looking for a stolen cab – some idiot went off with a taxi. He said I could turn around; I know another road into town, and I'm behind schedule.'

He turned the van into the opposite lane, which was empty of traffic, concentrating on turning the large vehicle in the small space.

Cassie was glad Frank wasn't watching her face; she knew her relief must be obvious. Behind them, the policeman was motioning cars around the stalled car, speaking briefly to each driver. Thank goodness he hadn't gotten a good look at her.

Frank turned at the next crossroads and followed an even narrower road around curves and over steep hillsides until it led into the small town. Here he pulled up in front of another gas station, checked his list, and went to the back of the truck in his usual routine.

Cassie looked around. The town was very small, with a few shops, a café, and two churches on what appeared to be the only main street. At first she didn't see any signs of unusual activity, but then she spotted the sheriffs car pulled up in front of the first store. Were they searching for Seth? Had someone seen him?

As she watched, a second police car pulled up, and one man got out. A policeman in a blue uniform walked out from the store and they talked. Was it her imagination, or did they look animated, their shoulders tense with anticipation. Had they spotted Seth?

It was time for her to leave the van and strike out on her own. She suspected this was as close as she might get to the center of the search area.

Frank was still inside. She hated to answer any more questions. Thinking quickly, she pulled out her notebook and tore out one sheet. She wrote, 'Thanks for the ride; I can walk the rest of the way.'

He would think she was ungrateful, leaving without a proper thank-you, Cassie thought regretfully. But she had a hard time telling lies; she'd turn red, and her voice would waver. Frank would know something was wrong.

She left the note on the driver's seat, then hesitated, looking at the box of damaged snacks. Frank had said they were discards; surely he wouldn't mind if she took a few more. She put several packages into her pockets, then slipped out of the van. She walked around to the back of the station and went inside the ladies' room. She took her time, washing her face and hands and combing her hair, and finally peeked past the doorway.

The van was gone. Relieved, yet also feeling curiously lonely, Cassie walked back to the main street, looking around and trying to act as if she belonged here.

The policemen still stood together talking; one wore a khaki uniform with a state policeman's hat, another had a lighter uniform. Was there any way she could get close enough to hear what they were saying?

But even as she tried to think of a plan, one of the policeman turned and went back to his car. She saw him lift the receiver of his radio and speak into it, then listen intently. In a moment he replaced the receiver, then went back to say something to the other man. The younger officer nodded, and the first man got into his police car, revved the engine, and pulled quickly away.

Cassie felt a flicker of alarm. Had Seth been caught? Was it too late for her to find him? He'd be hauled off to jail, and she'd never have the chance to speak to him. Oh, Seth, I hope you're all right, she thought.

Without any plan at all, but unable to be still, she walked slowly down the street. From the corner of her eye, she watched the policeman. He was watching her, she thought, and for a moment her heart beat faster. Did he know about her, was he also looking for a runaway?

She paused in front of the tiny grocery and stared into the shop window; she could see him reflected in the glass. And he was definitely staring. But the way he watched her was more admiring than menacing. Cassie relaxed a little. He looked very young, hardly out of his teens.

Cassie turned back toward the street, and as she approached, she gathered all her courage and met his eye, smiling shyly.

He grinned back. He was young, all right, and his uniform badge said Sheriffs Department. He wasn't state police, after all.

'What's going on?' Cassie paused, looking at the police car at the side of the street. 'What are all the police doing out at once?'

The young deputy threw his shoulders back. 'Haven't you heard? Some fool stole a taxicab, and it's been spotted in this area.'

Cassie fought to hold on to her smile. She couldn't let her anger show, or her fear. She tried to think what Angela would say, how Angela would smile up at the deputy in her easy way. 'Oh, wow. Have they – you – found the thief?'

'We will, any time. I just heard that they've spotted the taxi, ditched in a creekbed,' he bragged, seeming to appreciate her widened eyes.

'Is he – is the thief in the taxi?' Cassie felt cold with fear. Was Seth hurt?

'Probably, they don't know for sure – a helicopter spotted it. Hard to hide a yellow cab, you know. Why on earth anyone would snatch one of those, heck, he was probably drunk,' the young deputy told her. 'You live around here?'

Cassie nodded, looking away from his interested gaze. 'Just up the road.'

'I haven't seen you before,' the young man told her.

Cassie wasn't sure if he was flirting or really questioning her. She shrugged. 'Haven't seen you, either,' she told him, trying to hold on to her smile, trying to sound lighthearted, with nothing on her mind except making eyes at young men.

He grinned again. 'I usually work over the other side of the county,' he explained. 'But they pulled all of us in on this one; boy, wish I could be there when they collar the guy. They left me here to watch this road, but he's not going to just walk into town, is he?'

Cassie wished he would, not to get caught, but just so she'd know Seth was all right.

But she nodded.

'Oh, I'm supposed to ask, not that it matters much now, you seen this guy around?' He took a folded sheet of paper from his pocket and flipped it open; it was a copy of the police sketch she'd seen on the television newscast.

Cassie had to stare at the drawing, pretend

that the face was nothing to her. She shook her head. 'Guess I'd better get home, it'll be dark soon.'

The young man looked disappointed. 'Yeah, guess so. Maybe I'll see you the next time I'm back this way?'

'Maybe,' Cassie told him. She forced herself to walk slowly on past him, though she had a sudden urge to run, to hide, to scream Seth's name aloud. Where could he be? Was he already in custody, being taken away in handcuffs?

She felt tears heavy behind her eyelids and blinked hard. She didn't want the young deputy to suspect something. But she couldn't flash a fake smile any longer. She trudged past the rest of the stores, a tiny drugstore, a minute barber-shop, then hesitated. Something looked famil-iar; what was teasing her memory?

Then it hit her. The church at the other end of the street was a squat brick building, without grace or pretension. But the church at this end was a white frame building with a tall spire and arched doors. It reminded her strongly of the church where she and Seth had first met, in the youth group meeting in the church hall next door.

The thought brought back so many memories that Cassie felt one tear slip out, then another. She thought of Seth's face, could almost feel his fingers gentle against her cheek, hear his voice calling her name. Oh, God, she thought. How can you take him away from me? Was it so bad, what we did? She heard her father's voice in answer, *hellfire and damnation*, and pushed the echo angrily away. I loved him, she argued fiercely. Oh, Seth.

She missed going to church so much. She missed the kind voices, the harmonious music, a minister who didn't yell and scream like her father, the feeling of peace that it had once brought her. Was the church open? Cassie wished for a few minutes of quiet where she could sit and think and cry and pray, and remember Seth; it seemed that all she was going to have was memories.

She walked up to the front double doors and touched the latch gently, but it didn't budge. Locked.

Sighing, Cassie turned to go, and – more vivid than any of her memories so far – she could almost hear Seth calling to her.

'Cassie!'

It sounded so real. Reluctant to leave, Cassie looked up and down the street, but the young deputy was leaning against the storefront, looking bored, and no one else was in sight.

She walked around the side of the church and soon spotted another, smaller door. She walked up and tried the knob, and it turned under her hand.

Holding her breath, not sure what drew her so strongly, Cassie walked inside. The church building was dim; the simple frosted-glass windows partially blocked the sunlight, and none of the interior lights was turned on. But the smell of furniture polish and candles and dead flowers reminded her of the churches she and her family had visited so briefly, before her father's uncontrollable belligerence had driven them on.

Surely it wouldn't be wrong to just sit in a pew for a moment; she wouldn't touch anything. Blinking back tears, Cassie moved blindly toward a bench.

'Cassie!'

The voice had to be real. She turned, gasping at what she saw. He was dirty, and his shirt was torn. His eyes were red and heavy with fatigue, and he had a scratch on his cheek.

Cassie had never seen such a beautiful sight.

'Seth!' She ran into his outstretched arms, still unable to believe he wasn't a dream. But the arms that held her were firm to her touch, though they trembled now from emotion and weariness.

For a long while, they clung together, the miracle of their reunion too deep for words. Cassie only wanted to hold him, feel sure that this was not an illusion born of loneliness and thwarted love. For a few minutes it was enough that he was here. Then the other memories returned, the armed policeman outside only a few yards away, the hordes of police cars still searching.

'Oh, Seth, what happened? Are you all right?'

She felt him nod, his chin against her cheek. They were wrapped so tightly together that he had to pull back a little to look into her face. 'Cassie, you don't hate me, do you? I know it was a crazy thing to do, but I had to find you – I didn't know if you were okay.'

She reached up to touch his face, wincing at the raw scratch on his cheek. 'Of course I don't hate you. I could never hate you, Seth. But you're in so much trouble; there are police everywhere.'

'I know. I almost got caught by a roadblock.' Seth's tone was grim. 'I kept turning into side roads, and finally the road ended and I ran into a creek. I left the cab – it was stuck in the mud, and I couldn't get it out – and walked. Last night I saw this church, and it reminded me of the first time we met –'

'Oh, me, too,' Cassie interrupted eagerly. 'That's why I wanted to come inside.'

He nodded and hugged her again. 'I saw you from the front window, but the glass isn't clear, and I wasn't sure it was you – I thought I must be imagining it.'

'But you called me,' Cassie said. 'I thought I was hearing things.'

'I couldn't help it, it was like seeing water after you've been in the desert for weeks,' Seth told her, his voice trembling. 'Oh, Cassie, you don't know how I've worried about you.'

He held her tightly, laying his head against her shoulder. Cassie was silent, amazed at his love and his need. She'd never expected anyone to care for her like this. Why had they found this miracle too young, too soon, when they weren't ready for a love so strong that it made everything else look small and slight by comparison? It wasn't fair, she thought. Was anything in life fair?

'I'm okay,' she told him, touching his blond hair gently. 'I was worried about you, sick with worry. Seth, we have to get out of here. They're still looking for you.'

He nodded. 'We can stay here till dark, then slip around the roadblocks.'

She shook her head. 'I think we should go, now. There's only one deputy sheriff here. If we wait, they'll search the taxi and know you're not there, and they'll likely start combing the town again.

Seth looked at her and frowned. 'You shouldn't go with me,' he said, very low, even while his grip on her shoulders tightened. 'It's too dangerous.'

Cassie opened her eyes wide. 'After all this, you think I'm just going to let you walk away, Seth Allen!'

He grinned reluctantly, the old crooked grin that made her heart melt. 'Stubborn, aren't you?'

She nodded. 'We go together, Seth. That's the way it should be.'

He leaned forward and kissed her lightly on the forehead. 'That's all I want from my life, Cassie, all I've wanted since I met you.'

She shut her eyes and relished the joy of his words, of his presence.

'Okay, let's go.'

Hand in hand, they made for the side door, but a noise outside made Seth pause and Cassie hold her breath.

Seth whispered, 'There's someone coming.'

Chapter 16

Dear Diary,
I've found Seth; it's still hard to believe. I was
so afraid that I'd never see him again. If there
was only some way to hold on to this moment
and keep the disasters away. I love him so much.

They were crouched inside a small closet,
waiting for the two middle-aged women who
were arranging flowers in the church to finish
and go away. Seth had found the closet earlier
when he prowled the church, looking for hiding
places in case he needed to get out of sight.
When they heard the footsteps, he pulled
Cassie, frozen with fear, inside as the voices had
come closer and closer to the side door.

Now they crouched uncomfortably on the
wooden floor, listening to the women chat as
they polished brass candlesticks and arranged
fresh flowers. After a few minutes, the fear had
subsided a little and the monotony and close-
ness of the closet had lulled Seth, still tired

after his nighttime trek, into an uneasy doze. He leaned against the wall, his head sagging forward, and slept. Cassie, too nervous to sleep, too aware of the women so close outside the closet door, had taken her notebook and pen out of her pocket. Writing in her notebook kept her from screaming with impatience and fear.

The police would be back as soon as they determined that Seth was neither in the taxi nor in the immediate area of the creek bed. Valuable time was slipping by; why didn't those women go away?

Instead, Cassie heard one woman say, her voice muffled by the closed door, 'That looks a little crowded, Millie. Do you want another vase? There should be more in the closet behind the vestry. Shall I get you one?'

Cassie sat up straighter, tension rippling through her body. She grabbed Seth's arm.

He woke, his expression startled, and opened his lips to speak.

Cassie pressed her hand over his mouth until memory returned to remind him of the need for silence. He looked at her and nodded, his brows knit with worry, his eyes questioning.

She motioned toward the outside, and the voices. What would they do if the woman opened the closet door? Cassie looked wildly around, but saw nothing new. She'd already catalogued the pair of ancient rubber boots, a sad-looking sweater on a hook, two boxes of candles, three assorted vases, cartons of church bulletins and Sunday school pamphlets. There was nowhere to hide.

She heard the footsteps approach, and her body ached with tension. Seth reached over to take her hand; Cassie gripped it tightly.

'I don't think so, Kate,' the other woman called, her voice faint. 'This will do. I need to get back and pick up Calvin from kindergarten; he has an appointment this afternoon at the dentist.'

The footsteps receded again, and Cassie drew a long, shuddering breath.

In another five minutes – which seemed a small eternity to Cassie as she sat hunched in the closet, clasping Seth's hand in a desperate grip – the women finally walked out of the church, shutting the door behind them.

They waited one more long minute. 'Let's take a look,' Seth whispered.

He turned the knob and pushed the closet door open an inch. Cassie could see nothing but a strip of red carpet. They waited, listening hard. But the church seemed empty.

'Come on,' Seth said, and they tiptoed out. Cassie felt cramped and awkward; she tried to walk softly. At the outer door they stopped again to listen, but Cassie heard nothing but a bird singing in a tree outside, and farther away a dog barking.

Seth looked tense as he opened the door and glanced out. Nodding to Cassie, he went out the door.

Cassie followed, afraid of further surprises. But the grassy side lawn was empty, and she saw no one on the street.

'The deputy is up there,' she whispered to Seth, and they headed the other way, around the back of the church into an alley, then on past a couple of frame houses.

Cassie wanted to run, but Seth held her back. 'We don't want to look suspicious,' he whispered.

Cassie nodded, but it was so hard to walk when everything inside her told her to run.

A dog barked. Seth tensed – she could feel his body go stiff – and Cassie's heart leapt. She looked over her shoulder and located the sound. 'He's on a chain,' she said, and felt Seth relax again. Still holding hands, they walked as quickly as they could past the last house.

Cassie looked back over her shoulder, but saw no one watching. Seth had done the same; he signaled with a gentle tug on her hand, and they ducked behind a thick fir tree, then began to climb. The hillside was rugged, covered with trees and undergrowth. Cassie was glad she wore jeans and a denim jacket and not her usual cotton dress. The branches whipped at her arms and stung her legs, even through the thick cloth. But they had no time to look for a more open path. With Seth ahead, sometimes reaching back to grab her hand and pull her upward, they climbed as quickly as they could.

When they were far enough away that the houses below looked small and quaint glimpsed through the treetops, they stopped to catch their breath.

Cassie had a catch in her side, and she sat on an outcropping of rock and pressed one hand to the ache under her rib cage. Puffing a little, she wondered how far they could get on foot, when the police had cars and Jeeps and helicopters. Yet, how could they give up?

'You okay?' Seth asked her, sounding weary, too, his chest rising and falling rapidly. She heard the strange whistling in his voice, and she tensed. She had heard that sound before.

'Seth, can you breathe?'

'It's the plants,' he whispered. 'Too many.' He began to wheeze, and Cassie stared at him in alarm.

'Where's your inhaler?'

He couldn't answer, the asthma attack was getting worse, and it bent him double as he gasped for air. He was reaching for his pocket, and Cassie pushed past his groping fingers, found the inhaler – it felt very light, oh, please

God, Cassie thought, don't let it run out now –
and she pushed it into his hand.

Seth put the inhaler into his mouth and tried
to breathe, while she watched helplessly. What
good did it do to elude the police if Seth's own
body betrayed him?

After a few anxious minutes, the attack subsided. Seth put the inhaler back in his pocket
and sat slumped on the rock slab, his eyes
watering from the force of his gasps. She
watched him rub one hand impatiently across
his face.

How he must hate this affliction, Cassie
thought, which seemed to strike at the worst
times.

'Are you okay now?'

He nodded, but he didn't seem to trust his
voice yet. Cassie sat close beside him and took
his hand, and he put his other arm around her
shoulders. For a moment or two they sat
together silently.

Cassie watched the quiet landscape below. It
would not be quiet for long. Sooner or later,
probably sooner, the policemen would return,
with reinforcements. She shivered at the
thought. Seth would never make it over the
mountain on foot. And she couldn't leave him;
besides, where would she go? She had no place
to go back to. Her parents didn't want her; she
was in trouble at the girls' home after running

away – Lord knew what the courts would do to her now. She remembered Angela's ominous comments.

There was no going back, and little chance of going forward. Cassie felt the weight of fear and hopelessness return to her shoulders, lifted so briefly by their miraculous reunion. She held Seth's hand tightly, wanting to put her head against his shoulder and cry and cry. But she kept her tears inside with great effort; it was about the only thing she could do for Seth right now.

But just as she decided that their flight was useless, he tightened his grip on her hand. 'I know you're tired, but can you go on, now?' he said very softly.

She looked at him in surprise. 'Can you do it? Can you breathe? What about –'

He nodded, his face pale but determined. He took a bandanna out of his pocket and tied it across his face; it made him look suddenly foreign, frightening. If anyone saw him, they would think he really was a criminal, Cassie thought, and the notion made her want to cry all over again.

'I did this last night,' he told her, his voice muffled. 'Forgot to do it today, rushing to get away from town. It helps a little.'

She could see only his eyes; she focused on his familiar blue eyes, always warm, always full of love for her. 'If you're okay, I'm ready,' she told him.

She stood up awkwardly, and with Seth holding her hand, they climbed up the steep hillside.

Beneath the enveloping greenery, the air was warm and still. Cassie soon felt perspiration dampening her face and trickling down her back. She wanted to take off her jacket, but it protected her arms from the branches and briers; she unzipped it and let it hang open for coolness. Her hair was damp and glued to her forehead; she pushed the wisps back impatiently. Seth must be stifling under the bandanna mask, but as long as it helped his breathing, she knew he would keep it on.

The forest smelled musty. The remnants of last fall's foliage, once bright leaves now sodden and aged into a layer of thick mulch, muffled their footsteps. A twig poked Cassie under her ear, and she ducked. They pushed past another branch with its spring leaves just unfurling, like bright flags heralding a season of hope. Cassie saw little hope for the two of them.

The hillside seemed to slant upward forever, and she had no idea where they were going – did Seth? She was afraid to ask, afraid they were wandering in a featureless forest with no destination in sight, two desperate runaways with nowhere to go and no one who cared but each other.

Her side was hurting again; she slowed her steps, pressing one hand to her ribs.

Seth looked back at her. 'You okay? Need to rest a minute?'

'I'm sorry,' she murmured, near tears at her body's weakness. 'I'm slowing you down; maybe you should go on without me.'

The impatience in his face faded; Seth put both hands on her shoulders. 'Cassie, without you, I have no reason to go on. I'd never leave you.'

But instead of reassurance, his words brought her a renewed wave of guilt. 'Without me, you wouldn't be in so much trouble, either. I never meant to ruin your life as well as my own, Seth. I'm sorry.'

'You're not to blame for anything that I did,' Seth told her fiercely. 'And we both made this baby; you didn't do it by yourself, did you? I should have thought about that; I should have known that we'd be better off waiting. It was my stupidity, Cassie, that got you thrown out of your own home. As for me, I didn't have much at home, anyhow. I didn't have much to lose. Loving you is worth anything that happens to me.'

She didn't believe it – what if he went to prison? Nothing could be worth that – but his words brought tears to her eyes. Just knowing that she was valued, cherished, as she had never been in her own family, touched an old emptiness deep inside her. His love, his loyalty, were like sunlight to an almost withered seed.

She touched his cheek gently above the cloaking bandanna. 'How's your breathing – you okay?'

He flushed, the skin around his eyes turning pink, and she wished she hadn't asked.

'I'm fine,' he told her. 'I won't let you down again, Cassie.'

That wasn't what she had meant at all. But as she tried to think of a way to explain that, a new sound made Seth tense.

Cassie heard it, too, and she gripped his hand tightly. 'What is it?'

'Helicopter.'

Cassie gasped. 'Is it police? Are they looking for us?'

There was no need for him to answer. Instead, he stood up quickly and pulled her to her feet. 'We have to find a place with some cover,' he told her.

They hurried on through the trees, Seth glancing often and fearfully up at the sky. Cassie scanned the blue sky past the treetops, too, wishing that it were summer with the trees in full leaf; no one would see them, then.

But the leaves were just opening, coloring the dark trunks with a cloud of pale green, and there were too many gaps in the forest.

Seth pulled her along, going as quickly up the rough hillside as he could. Staring upward, Cassie stumbled on the uneven ground. She caught Seth's arm to steady herself and hurried after him.

The helicopter's drone was coming closer. She was rigid with fear. She felt like a sheep being herded by wolves, running uselessly in circles while the predators approached ever closer, eager for the kill.

Then Seth muttered, 'Over there.' He pulled her toward the sheltering branches of a large fir tree. The evergreen had wide-reaching arms, and Seth dropped to his knees and motioned Cassie beneath the concealing limbs.

They crawled deep into the shadow of the tree and crouched close together. Cassie took gasping breaths, heard the faint whistle of Seth's breathing, and hoped he wouldn't have another attack.

The helicopter roared overhead; they had taken shelter just in time. Cassie's heart seemed to beat almost as loudly as the aircraft's noisy engine; she shuddered, wondering if they would be spotted through the branches.

'Don't move,' Seth whispered into her ear.

She couldn't have moved if she tried, Cassie thought. At least she had Seth beside her; she wasn't alone anymore. She held on to his jacket and lay her head on his shoulder as he put one arm around her, holding her tight.

His nearness steadied her; she shut her eyes and thought only of Seth, Seth's arm around her, Seth's breath on her cheek. Some of her panic faded and, when the helicopter moved away, the roar of its engine fading to an irritating hum, she took a deep breath.

Neither spoke for a time, it was enough to know that the immediate threat was past. Or was it?

Cassie realized that the helicopter couldn't have landed on the slanted, tree-covered hillside even if the men inside had suspected their presence. They might be calling for policemen on foot, however.

'Do you think they saw us?' Cassie asked at last.

'Don't think so,' Seth told her.

Cassie was not inclined to argue. She hoped it were true, that they had eluded the authorities one more time.

Seth moved out from the center of the tree, stopping at the tree's perimeter where they would be less cramped but still somewhat hidden from view.

Cassie crawled after him. Without speaking, they paused, and she leaned against him once more as they sat on the layer of needles covering the ground. This time, Cassie could rest without being tense with fear.

She looked past their evergreen hideout to

the thick forest around them. She saw dog-woods sprinkled with dainty white blossoms and a few spring wildflowers growing in a sunny patch between the trees. She heard a mocking-bird call, and farther away, the light tapping of a woodpecker. It was beautiful here, she thought, even idyllic, if only they weren't being hunted.

Was this how Adam and Eve had felt, alone in the garden of Eden with only plants and animals surrounding them, and God's glory beyond? Had those ancient ancestors loved as strongly, Cassie wondered, as she and Seth? The Bible suggested that Eden's couple had been childlike, but children grow up, feel stir-rings that men and women were created to feel.

But Adam and Eve had been shamed, had been thrown out of the garden. Just like Cassie, who'd always thought her father one step away from God. She should hate herself for what she'd done, hate Seth, too.

Yet, leaning against Seth's shoulder, feeling his gentle touch on her arm, she couldn't believe he was evil. She would not believe that their love was wrong. They should have waited, yes, she knew that now. But how they felt for each other had to be good, had to be clean and bright and wonderful. God knew about love, didn't he? Surely he could understand why Cassie and Seth loved each other. A hard kernel of guilt inside her eased a little, and Cassie blinked back tears. Swallowing hard, she felt Seth tighten his grip on her shoulders reassuringly, offering love without question.

Oh, Seth, she thought. Dearest Seth.

When the shadows grew longer, Seth released her gently. Cassie, who had been lulled almost to sleep, looked at him in inquiry. 'We have to go?'

He nodded. 'I want to take a look around, first. It's so hard to tell which way we're going.'

Cassie understood; the tall trees cloaked the outlines of the mountains, and even the sun was hard to see. She watched as Seth walked to a tall maple with a branch low enough for him to pull himself up. With effort, he pulled his body over the limb, then scrambled up to get a foothold. Reaching carefully for each branch, he climbed slowly upward. Cassie bit her lip, hoping he wouldn't fall. Near the top of the tree, he stopped to look in all directions, holding tightly to the trunk as he twisted for a better view.

At last he started back down. Cassie relaxed as he descended, dropping the last five feet to land with a thump on the ground. His eyes were sparkling; she looked at him in surprise. What had he seen?

'Come on,' he told her. 'I know where we're going, now.'

Chapter 17

Dear Cassie,

I guess it's silly to be writing this when you're lying right beside me. But looking at your face and your soft hair and watching you sleep fills me so full of love I have to write it down; even when you wake, I may not know the words to tell you. I'm so glad I found you, Cassie.

She was so beautiful, Seth thought, with her dark hair framing her face, one hand pillowed beneath her cheek. But the blue circles under her eyes, the lines of fatigue in her face, made something hurt inside him. Oh, Cassie, I just want to make everything okay for you, he thought. How am I going to do that?

They had shared the damaged snacks that Cassie had been carrying in her pockets, gulping down chocolate cupcakes and peanut-butter cookies. He'd insisted on giving most of the food to Cassie, assuring her that he wasn't very hungry, which wasn't true. But Cassie needed it more.

His stomach still felt empty and his throat was parched; he wished for a cold bottle of cola or just the good spring water he'd had at the farmhouse, anything to ease his dry throat, but they had nothing to drink.

Still, the light meal seemed to help Cassie, and then, her weariness plain, he'd convinced her to lie back on the grass and nap a little.

Seth had meant to stand guard, but as he watched her sleep, his eyes grew heavy, too, and he drifted off.

He woke to hear a rustle of paper. Opening his eyes, he blinked at the inky darkness. It was really night, now, with no city lights out here. He tensed, trying to see what had made the noise.

He felt Cassie stir beside him. 'What's wrong?' she whispered.

He murmured, 'Don't know; I heard something.'

Then a movement caught his eye, and Seth stared hard through the darkness. The night was quiet and cool, and he felt Cassie shiver; the grass was damp with dew and they were both going to be chilled. But what was on the mountainside with them?

He hoped it wasn't a bear. Did they still have bears in the Tennessee mountains?

Then a cloud slid past, and the moon's bright face reappeared. In the ghostly light, Seth saw an animal's form, but it was too small to be a bear, unless it was only a cub. But the shape didn't seem quite right.

'Is it a dog?' Cassie whispered. She was watching, too, as the animal tossed aside the paper that had covered their cupcakes, trying to find the food that it smelled on the discarded wrappers.

Something about the agility of the paws alerted him. Seth sighed in relief. 'No, it's just a raccoon.' He could see the dark eyes glittering in the black mask, now, and the stripes on the tail.

Cassie relaxed and spoke more loudly. 'Oh, good; I was worried.'

But the animal turned when it heard her voice and gave a menacing sound, between a growl and a hiss. Seth saw its sharp teeth bared and decided that this thing wasn't all that small, after all.

'Come on,' he said. 'Let's get away from this coon – no sense risking trouble.'

He'd meant to clean up the paper they had left, but he wasn't fighting a raccoon for it; the animal wanted any crumbs left on the wrappings.

They backed away. Cassie stumbled over a tree root, and Seth grabbed her quickly.

'Seth, where are we going?'

'I think I know a place to hide for a little

while,' Seth told her. She had told him about the roadblocks. Seth still found it hard to realize that so many people were looking for him. He hadn't meant to cause so much turmoil, hadn't planned on hijacking a taxi or kidnapping its driver. Kidnapping was a very serious crime; Seth thought about spending the rest of his life in prison, and the darkness inside him seemed heavier than the cloudy night outside. He tried to push the thought away. He had to get Cassie to safety, then he'd worry about it all, later.

It was hard to walk in the darkness. The moon went in and out of the clouds, and the trees overhead blocked some of the moonlight. The ground beneath them was littered with branches and pinecones, and they stumbled often over the rough ground. Once Seth heard a faraway howl, and he shivered.

They had to duck under a low-hanging branch. Seth pulled back a branch to allow Cassie to go ahead. But she stopped abruptly.

'Oh!' Cassie waved her hands in dismay.

'What's wrong?' Seth hurried to catch up. Then, he, too, felt the filmy web sticking to his face. 'It's just a cobweb, Cassie.'

'But there may be~oh!' She shrieked at the movement on her arm.

Seth moved quickly as the large arachnid ran up her arm toward her shoulder; he knocked the big spider away. It dropped to the ground and skittered off into the shadows.

Cassie ran forward, away from the tree and the web. She rubbed frantically at her body, trying to pull the rest of the spiderweb off her face and arms. She was crying.

'Cassie, it's okay now.'

'Make sure there aren't any more,' she begged him, still shivering. 'I hate spiders, I hate them.'

He looked as carefully as he could in the dim moonlight, brushing her cheeks lightly to help rid her of the sticky web, running his hands down her arms and chest and back. Then he put his arms around her as she leaned against him, sobbing.

'It's okay,' he murmured.

Howling echoed behind them, eerie in the darkness. Seth tensed. Was the sound closer, or was it only his fear that made it seem so?

'We have to get moving, Cassie,' he told her softly. 'When the moon goes down, it's going to be really dark.'

She raised her head from his shoulder, looked at the moon and the clouds floating past its pale face. A gust of wind moved her dark hair, and Seth thought again how beautiful she was.

Cassie nodded. 'Okay,' she said. 'I'm sorry I was so silly.'

'You're never silly,' he told her gruffly, love

constricting his throat when he thought how brave she was, how hard she was trying to keep up when he could see the weariness in every step she made. But he couldn't tell her that, either. 'I love you, Cassie.'

'I love you, too.' She returned his hug, then they stepped reluctantly apart, and he took her hand and led her into the darkness.

For half an hour they made their way beneath the trees, and Seth thought – prayed – he was still leading them in the right direction. And then he heard the dogs again.

'Seth!' Cassie seemed to really notice the echoing howls for the first time. 'What was that?'

'A pack of wild dogs, I think,' Seth said grimly, trying to keep his voice calm. No need to show how his heart jumped when he heard that fearsome sound, no need to frighten Cassie.

'But they sound so close.'

He nodded, not sure he should tell her that he thought the dogs were coming closer, too. Were they tracking Seth and Cassie?

The idea of savage dogs hot on their trail made Seth shiver despite himself.

'You don't think they're dangerous, do you?' Cassie asked him.

'I don't know,' Seth told her, not sure whether to be totally honest or not. 'But we'd better hurry.'

She followed him as he stepped up the pace, but it was easier said than done in the dark forest. They stumbled more often over tree roots and rocks and clumps of grass. Then the ground dipped suddenly in front of them, and Seth couldn't stop in time. His feet slid out from under him and he slid down the embankment. He hit the bottom with a thud, grunting with the impact.

'Are you okay?' Cassie called anxiously from above.

Seth pushed himself up, grunting at the pain of his scrapes and bruises. 'Yeah, I think so. Stay there.'

The ground was so steep that he had to crawl back up. When he got to the top, Cassie reached anxiously to help. Seth took her hand and pulled himself to his feet; when he straightened, he discovered that his right ankle throbbed with pain when he put all his weight on it. Could he walk?

The dogs howled again, louder and nearer.

'Oh, Seth!' Cassie's eyes were wide; she seemed to have no doubt about their danger now. Something in the wildness of the sound, the ferocity and feralness of it, destroyed any picture she might have had of docile, tail-wagging pets.

These dogs had put away their hearthside manners. Thrust painfully out of their homes, they were wild things now: forest animals, savage and deadly.

This was what happened when the rules were broken, Seth thought, even as he and Cassie exchanged fearful glances.

Seth gritted his teeth. He had to get moving. When Cassie saw his pain, she looked even more worried. She stopped and bent over.

He thought for an instant she was sick herself, then saw that she was feeling along the ground.

'I thought I saw – here, Seth, try this.' It was a long, almost straight branch.

Seth broke off the twigs at the end, and the piece of wood gave him something to lean on. He limped heavily, but the stick helped. They set off again, traveling as quickly as they could.

It was hard to know if they were still going north. He wished he could check their direction, but doubted he could climb a tree with his weakened ankle.

Then Cassie gasped, and Seth looked over his shoulder. He had heard it, too, the rapid patter of running feet. The dogs were closing in.

Seth looked around for a tree with branches low enough to climb. 'Over here,' he called, stumbling toward a sturdy maple.

'What?' Cassie blinked at him, not understanding.

He dropped the stick and made a stirrup with

his hands. 'Quick, get up in the tree. Hurry, Cassie.

She hesitated, then stepped into his hand, and he pushed her toward the tree limb. She grasped it, swung perilously for an instant, then, with him pushing from below, managed to obtain a shaky seat on the limb.

'Aren't you coming?' Her voice quivered.

He didn't have time to explain that with his almost useless ankle, he didn't think he could climb. He heard the rush of padded feet behind him and turned quickly.

The dog in front was large with shaggy fur; Seth couldn't tell the color in the fading moonlight. The animal looked as if it could have been a mixture of shepherd and lab; it stood as high as his hip, and its coat was rough and matted.

Behind the leader was the rest of the pack – four or five, Seth thought, afraid to risk a long look. He couldn't take his eyes away from the first dog, which stood only a few feet away, watching him.

The dog's eyes glittered in the darkness. Seth couldn't tear his gaze away to look at the sky, but he knew the moon was sinking fast. When the moonlight was gone, they would be alone in the darkness with these creatures.

Seth felt as if he were hypnotized; the dog's eyes were bright and menacing and supremely confident as it growled low in its throat. It was the boss here, the pack leader, and it didn't expect any real resistance from its prey.

Seth's stomach knotted with fear, and he felt lightheaded. The dog growled again, pulling back its lips to show the large teeth, and the sound ran down Seth's back like icy water. He hoped he wouldn't pass out.

Then he heard Cassie move in the tree above him, and instinctively he squared his shoulders. It wasn't just him, it was Cassie he was protecting.

He wished he had his stick, but he was afraid to bend over to search the ground for it.

The dog snarled again and stepped closer.

'Don't do it, Buster,' Seth told it, trying to sound more confident than he felt. 'Keep your distance!'

Another dog circled around him, then leapt for the branch that Cassie perched on. He heard her gasp and hug the tree.

But he had half turned, afraid for her, and from the corner of his eye, he saw the lead dog take another step forward. Its hind legs gathered for the leap, even as Cassie called, 'Look out!'

The dog sprang for his throat. Seth threw up one arm, received the weight of the heavy animal against his forearm, felt the rending teeth tear his flesh. He fell heavily backward from the impact, the dog still on top of him.

Cassie screamed.

Seth grabbed the lead dog by the throat, holding off the heavy body, pushing it back so that the snarling mouth with the sharp teeth couldn't reach his throat or his face. But it took all Seth's strength to hold the big dog away, and he was helpless to stop the rest of the pack.

The other dogs rushed forward, they were darting in and out, biting at him, worrying his legs and his arms, one coming all too close to his face. Seth felt their hot, sour breath on his cheeks and heard the cacophony of snarls and barks.

He was beyond thinking, planning, he could see only the glittering eyes and snapping teeth, feel the sharp pains as they ripped his jeans and his jacket to get to his skin and taste blood.

All he could hear was the sound of the pack, so he wasn't prepared to see the thick branch swinging from behind him, above him, attacking the dogs. Cassie!

Seth glimpsed her face, contorted with fear and rage, tears on her cheeks as she swung the piece of wood; he heard it thudding against the dogs' bodies.

The animals snarled, but they backed away a little, and Seth could concentrate on the dog he still held between his two hands. With one final desperate burst of strength, he choked the dog until it coughed and gasped and seemed to lose strength. Then Seth threw the heavy body away from him. The dog landed limply, then while Seth watched, waiting for another attack, the animal pulled itself to its feet, breathing hoarsely.

The pack leader backed away, its eyes glinting as it watched them, whining a little now from the pain of its struggle. It stopped at the edge of the little clearing, snarled once, but without real conviction, then turned and trotted away into the trees. The other dogs followed silently. Seth took a deep breath; he couldn't believe they were gone, and he and Cassie were still alive. He'd thought they would die there, alone in the forest.

Cassie grabbed him, sobbing. 'Seth, you're bleeding!'

He put his arm around her, held her while she clung to him, not sure that his face wasn't also damp. Shuddering, he held her tight.

They stood for a moment, gaining strength from each other, then Seth raised his head. Beyond the tree – yes, that was what he'd been following. The tall radio tower rose above the trees, a blinking light at its top shining against the dark sky.

He could feel all his wounds hurting, now; he felt weak and sick. How much blood had he lost? His tattered jeans were sticky with it, and his arms stung with pain.

He took Cassie's hand. 'We have to find shelter. They might come back.'

Trembling, she nodded, and they set out again.

Chapter 18

Dear Diary,

We found the radio tower and followed the trail until we located the cabin. Seth was bleeding and could hardly walk, and I was afraid the dogs would come back.

Seth forced up one of the windows and climbed in. The cabin is small and rustic, but there's a spring up the hill. We found a first-aid kit and candles and matches, and I cleaned and bandaged his wounds the best I could; I think some of them need stitches.

I know he's in pain. Poor Seth. How did we come to be in such a mess? All we wanted to do was to see each other sometimes. I love him so much. But now Seth's hurt; he's in trouble with the law, and so am I. And there's the baby . . . what are we going to do about the baby?

Cassie put down her pen and sighed. Seth was sleeping on one of the bunks built into the wall. She had dozed awhile in the next bunk, but soon woke; too many worries still ran through her mind.

The cabin had seemed like a wonderful refuge when they finally found it, sitting back from the little trail. Cassie had wondered aloud at the discovery, until Seth explained about the old lady in the farmhouse farther down the hill who had mentioned the cabin to him earlier.

He liked the old lady, Cassie could tell. He had tried hard not to do any real damage to the window, but they couldn't pass up shelter, especially with the pack of dogs still roaming the forest.

Now daybreak washed the sky outside the window with streaks of color. Cassie put aside her notebook and pen and blew out the candle. She visited the outhouse out back, came back and washed her hands in the tin basin, then explored the cabin more thoroughly.

Besides the narrow bunks, there was a table and three chairs, a camp stove and a small cupboard against one wall. Cassie opened it, thrilled to see cans of food. Was there a can opener? Yes, and an assortment of utensils and plastic plates, matches, even a pot or two.

She picked out a can of soup, took the pail they had found, and went back outside to get more water, then came back, opened a window, and lit the propane stove. By the time Seth stirred and opened his eyes, she had soup heated and had even wiped the dust off the little table and set it for a meal.

Seth blinked and sat up in the bunk.

Cassie waited as he looked around, hoping he wouldn't laugh. She had picked wildflowers behind the cabin and put them in an old mason jar in the center of the table. The spoons and bowls were set out neatly, and she'd even found some paper napkins.

'I made you some soup,' she said. 'How do you feel?'

'Not too bad. It smells good, and the table looks real pretty.'

She smiled shyly at him. When they first fell in love, she had daydreamed about getting married someday, about having their own home. The thought of spending every day with Seth made happiness well up inside her. But now they would never – no, she pushed that thought away.

'Come eat your soup,' she told him, feeling almost like a real wife. He sat down at the table and she poured the steaming soup into bowls. Seth waited till she seated herself, then grinned at her.

'This is perfect.'

She flushed slightly, watching him slowly spoon up the hot soup. They ate slowly, and for a little while, Cassie didn't think of anything outside this cabin. If they could just keep the rest of the world away . . .

'Did you sleep?' he asked her.

'Some,' she told him. 'I kept having nightmares about those dogs. Did you?'

He shook his head. 'I was bitten by a dog when I was little; did I ever tell you that?'

'Oh, Seth.' She lowered her spoon to look at him.

'It was just a little peke, but I wasn't very big, either. I never cared much for dogs after that. I used to walk a whole block out of the way, just to avoid going past a yard with a dog in it.'

'That must have made it even worse when those dogs attacked. I was so scared; I thought you'd be killed.'

'So did I.' Seth grinned ruefully at her. 'But you know, last night I didn't dream about them at all. It's like having your worst nightmare come true, and you can't ever be so afraid again.'

She felt tears in her eyes and had to blink hard. 'Seth, we have to talk.'

'Not now.' He shook his head quickly, bent back over his soup. 'Let me enjoy being with you for a little while, Cassie. I don't want to think about anything else; just the nice vegetable soup which tastes so good, and four walls around us, and you beside me. That's all I need.'

She blinked again, and had to swallow hard before she could finish her own soup.

Then Seth limped outside to the outhouse,

and Cassie washed the dishes in cold water in the plastic dishpan and put everything neatly away back in the cupboard. She found a garbage bag and put the empty can and paper napkins in it, then swept out the cabin.

When Seth came back, he sat down on the edge of the bunk, and she went to sit beside him. He put one arm around her shoulders, and they sat in silence for a while. Just to be together, Cassie thought. It didn't seem so much to ask.

She felt so safe with his arm around her, sitting so close. She leaned against him and felt the comforting warmth of his body through his T-shirt and torn jeans.

Too warm. Cassie touched his face. 'You're hot,' she said sharply. 'You've got a fever, Seth. You need to get to a doctor.'

He shook his head. 'I don't want a doctor; I just want you. I'd rather stay here.'

'We can't, Seth. Those dog bites could become infected. You could even have rabies – that would kill you!' Her voice rose as she thought of the dangers. 'I couldn't stand that.'

'But I don't want to leave yet. Can't we stay awhile?' he asked her, his voice low.

Cassie bit her lip. She wanted to agree, wanted to stay in this playhouse with him. But Seth's face was too pale, and his eyes glittered with fever. She couldn't risk his life. And besides

– 'Seth,' she said slowly. 'This is all pretend. We can't stay in the cabin with only a few cans of soup and you hurt and the police still looking for us. They'll find us eventually. You need to turn yourself in; maybe that would be better for you.'

'But I wanted to help you, Cassie,' Seth told her. 'I wanted to get you away from that place.'

'Seth, it's okay. McNaughten's not so bad; I think I can be happier there than I was at home. At least my father's not there to make everyone miserable,' Cassie tried to explain. 'And I can go to school; I like going to school. One of my teachers even said I should think about college, but I don't think I can, with the baby . . .' She took a deep breath. 'Seth, we have to talk about the baby.'

He put his hand lightly over her abdomen. 'Look, I felt him move again. Or her. It's wonderful, Cassie. I can hardly believe it, your baby and mine. Ours.'

Cassie wanted to cry. His voice was soft, and his touch tender. But she made herself speak.

'How are we going to take care of a baby, Seth?'

'I'll get a job, I'll –'

'Seth, you haven't even finished high school. What can you do? How can you make enough money? And anyhow, you won't have a chance. You're going to be in jail.'

He flushed, and she felt as guilty as if she'd struck him. 'I'm sorry, Seth, but you know they're not going to ignore the things you've done. Taking the taxi, hijacking the driver. I know you wanted to find me, but it's not right, Seth. What if it had been you, with a wife and children at home. How would you feel? How would I have felt?'

He looked down at the rough planks of the floor. 'I know. Do you hate me, Cassie?'

'I'd never hate you.' She reached for his hand and pressed it to her cheek; his skin felt hot against her face. He needed medical attention. Time was running out; time was always running out for them. 'But I know they're going to take you away; and I'll have to go back to McNaughten. They're not going to forget about me, either.'

If she didn't have to go somewhere worse. Cassie thought about Angela's warning, about the penalties for escape, and hoped that it wouldn't go too hard on her. But she didn't want to tell Seth that part; he had enough to worry about.

'So if you're somewhere locked up and I'm locked up somewhere else, how can we take care of a baby? Our baby deserves better than that, Seth.'

'You want to give it away?' His eyes were accusing. 'Just like that?'

Cassie couldn't look at him; she jumped up and paced up and down across the cabin floor. 'I don't want to, I just want it to have a real home and a family. I saw Angela and her baby, and it's so hard to do it right, Seth, all by yourself. And I don't have anyone to help me; my family won't take me in, and I wouldn't want a baby to grow up with my father, anyhow. I suffered enough.'

'I want to help you, Cassie,' Seth said.

She couldn't bear to look at him; the pain in his eyes was too great.

'But you won't be there,' she said, leaning over the table, feeling sick at the thought. 'If we both sign, the baby could go to a real home –'

'I can't do it, Cassie,' Seth told her. For the first time, he raised his voice, almost shouting. 'My dad walked out on me; I swore I'd never do that. I won't give up my baby. Maybe you can do it, but I won't!'

Stung, she swung back to glare at him. 'I never said it's what I wanted to do, Seth. I'm trying to think about what's best for the baby.'

He took a deep breath and let it out slowly. 'It's too hard, Cassie. I'm trying to think about the baby, too, but I don't think I can let it go. It's my baby.'

His eyes were so bright they frightened her, and even his voice was weaker.

'Will you think about it, at least?' she asked him. 'Please, Seth?'

He nodded slowly. She went to him and touched his face. 'I'm going to have to go for help for you, Seth. I'll try to find that farmhouse and the old lady. She has a phone?'

'I think so,' Seth muttered. 'Cassie, I wish we'd had more time. Will you wait for me, if it's not too long, I mean? I hope it won't be too long.'

She could hear his uncertainty. How many years would it be, before both of them were free? She felt the same panic, the same fear, and she hugged him tightly. 'I'll try, Seth. I love you. You know I love you.'

He kissed the side of her face, ran his finger lightly down her cheek. 'I love you, too, Cassie. Always.'

She touched his hand, then stepped back, gathering her courage.

He stood up awkwardly. 'I'm going with you.'

'I don't think you can walk that far,' she told him anxiously. 'We don't know how far down the road it is.'

'I won't let you go alone,' he told her. 'The dogs might come back. And anyhow, we'll have a little while longer to spend together. I don't want to waste a minute.'

They shut the door carefully on the cabin and walked slowly down the trail. Seth leaned a little on her arm.

The day was bright, the sky a pale blue, and

the sunshine golden. Birds flitted and called in the trees that overhung the narrow road, and Cassie saw a fat robin with a beak full of straw. Nest building, she thought. Spring meant love and little ones to raise.

The pain was so great, she thought her heart might really break, just like all the songs said. She blinked hard. She wouldn't cry now when Seth needed all his strength; she wouldn't upset him any further.

She would try to remember the feel of his arm around her, the touch of his hand against her cheek, their time in the little cabin and their after-school meetings. She had to hold on to the bright moments against all the pain and the loss they had faced and still had to endure. Sometime, surely, beyond the coming separation, there must be another golden day when both of them would be old enough, free enough, prepared enough that love could grow unfettered.

'They can't take away what we've had, Seth,' she told him. 'Nor what we have between us. No one can make us stop loving.'

He squeezed her hand; his face was pale. She knew it was taking all his effort just to stay erect.

They walked slowly side by side along the narrow road, and they had climbed the next hill before they spotted the police car.

SAPLING ORDER FORM

☐	0 7522 0669 9	Apollo 13 Junior Novelisation	£3.99 pb
☐	0 7522 0145 X	Hollyoaks: Coming Together	£3.50 pb
☐	0 7522 0247 2	Starfiles	£4.99 pb

Blossom:

☐	0 7522 0926 4	Family Album	£3.99 pb
☐	0 7522 0931 0	Trouble with Secrets	£2.99 pb

California Dreams:

☐	0 7522 0906 X	Perfect Harmony	£3.50 pb
☐	0 7522 0916 7	Playing for Keeps	£3.50 pb
☐	0 7522 0911 6	Who Can You Trust	£3.50 pb

Saved By The Bell:

☐	0 7522 0623 0	Bayside Madness	£3.50 pb
☐	0 7522 0618 4	California Scheming	£3.50 pb
☐	0 7522 0901 9	Girl's Night Out	£3.50 pb
☐	0 7522 0608 7	Kelly's Hero	£3.50 pb
☐	0 7522 0613 3	Ol' Zack Magic	£3.50 pb
☐	0 7522 0995 7	One Wild Weekend	£3.50 pb
☐	0 7522 0990 6	Zack's Last Scam	£3.50 pb
☐	0 7522 0985 X	Zack Strikes Back	£3.50 pb
☐	0 7522 0181 6	Impeach Screech	£3.50 pb
☐	0 7522 0191 3	Don't Tell a Soul	£3.50 pb
☐	0 7522 0196 4	Computer Confusion	£3.50 pb
☐	0 7522 0186 7	Silver Spurs	£3.50 pb
☐	0 7522 0918 3	Scrapbook	£3.50 pb

Saved By The Bell – New Class:

☐	0 7522 0670 2	Breaking the Rules	£3.50 pb
☐	0 7522 0665 6	Going, Going, Gone	£3.50 pb
☐	0 7522 0660 5	Spilling the Beans	£3.50 pb
☐	0 7522 0655 9	Trouble Ahead	£3.50 pb

Tomorrow People:

☐	0 7522 0637 0	The Culex Experiment	£3.99 pb
☐	0 7522 0642 7	Monsoon Man	£3.99 pb
☐	0 7522 0652 4	The Living Stones	£3.99 pb
☐	0 7522 0647 8	Rameses Connection	£3.99 pb

All these books are available at your local bookshop or can be ordered direct from the publisher. Just tick the titles you want and fill in the form below.

Prices and availability subject to change without notice.

Boxtree Cash Sales, P.O. Box 11, Falmouth, Cornwall TR10 9EN

Please send a cheque or postal order for the value of the book and add the following for postage and packing:

U.K. including B.F.P.O. – £1.00 for one book plus 50p for the second book, and 30p for each additional book ordered up to a £3.00 maximum.

Overseas including Eire – £2.00 for the first book plus £1.00 for the second book, and 50p for each additional book ordered.

OR please debit this amount from my Access/Visa Card (delete as appropriate).

Card Number ☐☐☐☐☐☐☐☐☐☐☐☐☐☐☐☐☐☐

Amount £ ....

Expiry Date ....

Signed ....

Name ....

Address ....

WIN A CD MICRO-SYSTEM

Are you all cried out?
Well here's something to cheer you up!

We've got a fantastic Amstrad Micro 1000 Hi-Fi System to give away when you enter our competition. Features include a CD player with 21 track programmability, a cassette deck with recording LED and autostop, medium and FM wavebands, remote control and matching speakers.
Five runners-up will each receive a £20 CD voucher.

To enter collect all four tokens found in the following *Tear Jerkers* novels:
Token 1 - Runaway • Token 2 - Remember Me
Token 3 - Family Secrets • Token 4 - Once in a Blue Moon
and complete the tie-breaker below.

Send them with your name and address to: Tear Jerkers Competition, Boxtree Limited, 2nd Floor Broadwall House, 21 Broadwall, London SE1 9PL.
Closing Date is 30th September 1996.

- -

ENTRY FORM

Complete the following tie-breaker in an apt and original way, using no more than 10 words. "I love a good cry with 'Tear Jerkers' because ....
....

Name ....

Address ....

.... Postcode ....

Signature of Parent/Guardian (If under 16 yrs) ....

> **Tear Jerkers
> Competition
> TOKEN**
>
> **1**

RULES

1. The competition is open to all residents of the British Isles, other than employees of Boxtree Ltd or their advertising agents. Parental consent is needed if entrant is younger than 16 years.
2. Only entries on the official entry form accompanied by all four tokens will be accepted (photocopies not accepted). Only 1 entry per household.
3. The prize will be awarded in order of merit to the entrants who, in the opinion of the judges, have completed the tie-breaker in the most apt and original way. The first prize is an Amstrad Micro 1000 Hi-Fi. The five runners-up will each receive a £20 CD voucher. No cash alternatives to the prize.
4. Winners will be notified by post by 30th October 1996 and the prize will be dispatched by recorded delivery after this date.
5. The judges decision will be final and no correspondence will be entered into. No responsibility will be taken for entries lost or damaged in the post.
6. For a list of judges, winners and results send a S.A.E. to the competition address before 1st November 1996.
7. Closing date 30th September 1996.

...tition Registration No: 654
...Boxtree Ltd, 2nd Floor Broadwall House, 21 Broadwall, London SE1 9PL.